SHATTERED MIRROR

Also by Amelia Atwater-Rhodes

In the Forests of the Night

Demon in My View

SHATTERED MIRROR

AMELIA ATWATER-RHODES

DELACORTE PRESS

Published by
Delacorte Press
an imprint of
Random House Children's Books
a division of Random House, Inc.
1540 Broadway
New York, New York 10036

The trademark Delacorte Press® is registered in the U.S. Patent and
Trademark Office and in other countries.

Visit us on the Web! www.randomhouse.com/teens
Educators and librarians, for a variety of teaching tools, visit us at
www.randomhouse.com/teachers

Library of Congress Cataloging-in-Publication Data

Atwater-Rhodes, Amelia.
    Shattered mirror / by Amelia Atwater-Rhodes.
        p.   cm.
    Summary: As seventeen-year-old Sarah, daughter of a powerful line of
vampire-hunting witches, continues to pursue the ancient bloodsucker
Nikolas, she finds herself in a dangerous friendship with two vampire
siblings in her high school.
    ISBN 0-385-32793-5 (hardcover)
    1. Youths' writings, American.   [1. Vampires—Fiction.   2. Witches—
Fiction.   3. Youths' writings.]   I. Title.

PZ7.A8925 Sh 2001
[Fic]—dc21

                                                        2001023509

The text of this book is set in 12-point Cochin.
Book design by Saho Fujii

Manufactured in the United States of America

September 2001

10 9 8 7 6 5 4 3

Dedicated to Carolyn Barns, who knows these characters as well as I do, understands all my vague references and odd humor, and can push me on when I've all but given up. Carolyn, I owe you.

As always I must mention my family, especially my sister Gretchen. Thank you for believing in me, for listening to my dreams.

My love to Indigo of the Round Table. Carolyn, Sydney, Irene, and Valerie, where would I be without you all? You—and Alexandre, and TSB, and Londra, and Hawk, and Ysterath, and even the evil fairy (whom I never liked even if he was a good guy)—are the people who make my life interesting.

More thanks go to the members of the Rikai Group for all their encouragement and support while I was editing Shattered Mirror. *My deepest gratitude goes to Kyle Bladow, who believed in me even when I didn't, and to Darrin Kuykendall, who showed me how to put water on my cereal while I waited for the milk.*

Last but not least, thanks to my editor, Diana. Without her suggestions and comments, this book would never have become what it is today.

The Two Trees

Beloved, gaze in thine own heart.
Gaze no more in the bitter glass
The demons, with their subtle guile.
Lift up before us when they pass,
Or only gaze a little while;
For there a fatal image grows
That the stormy night receives,
Roots half hidden under snows,
Broken boughs and blackened leaves.
For ill things turn to barrenness
In the dim glass the demons hold,
The glass of outer weariness,
Made when God slept in times of old.
There, through the broken branches, go
The ravens of unresting thought;
Flying, crying, to and fro,
Cruel claw and hungry throat,
Or else they stand and sniff the wind,
And shake their ragged wings; alas!
Thy tender eyes grow all unkind:
Gaze no more in the bitter glass.

W. B. Yeats

CHAPTER I

SARAH VIDA SHIVERED. The aura of vampires seeping from the house in front of her was nearly overwhelming. She drove around the block once, then stopped her car a couple of yards away from the white Volvo she had been following. Her sapphire Jaguar was flashy, and she hadn't had time to change the plates.

She was lucky she had been planning on crashing a different party, or she would never have been ready for this one. She had come across the white Volvo's owner at a gas station and had tailed her here.

She cut the motor and ran her fingers

through her long blond hair, which was windblown by the drive in the convertible. Flashing a killer smile at no one, she checked her appearance in the rearview mirror. The girl in the glass appeared attractive, wild and carefree. The core of stone was not visible in her reflection.

As she stood, Sarah smoothed down her blue tank top and cream jeans and automatically checked to make sure her knives were in place—one in a spine sheath on her back and one tucked into each calf-high boot. Only then did she approach the house.

With blinds and shades pulled, the house appeared empty from the outside, but the illusion was quickly shattered. Before she even had a chance to knock, someone pulled open the door.

Leech, Sarah thought, disgusted, as she flashed a smile as practiced as the one she had given her rearview mirror at the vampire who had opened the door.

Whoa. Her smile did not waver, even though the vampiric aura in the house hit her like a sledgehammer to her gut. Her skin tingled at the sense of power, the feeling as unpleasant as sandpaper scraping across raw skin.

Unpleasant feeling or no, she began to mingle, looking always for the prey she was risking her neck to find—Nikolas.

Nikolas was one of the most infamous of his kind, a vampire who had hunted blatantly since the 1800s. His first known prey had been a young mother named Elisabeth Vida. Elisabeth had been a witch, a vampire hunter, and incidentally, Sarah's ancestor. Her family had been hunting Nikolas ever since—without success.

Nikolas was clever—he had to be to have eluded hunters from the most powerful family of witches for so long. But he was also vain, and that would be his downfall. Every one of his victims wore his marks, decorations cut into their arms with the blade of his knife. Nikolas allowed some of his victims to live, but he twisted their minds to make them sickeningly loyal to him. Hunters had caught more than one of those warped humans, but they each professed to choose death before they would betray the vampire.

One of them, however, had made a mistake. A flat tire on the way to this bash had left her fuming at a gas station off Route 95, and she had been too preoccupied to cover the scars on her arms. The attendant, a member of the hunters' complex system of informants, had called Sarah; she had followed the girl's white Volvo here.

Taking a breath to focus her senses, Sarah searched the room with all six of them. Human scents mingled with the overpowering aura of vampires. Sarah felt pity and a slight disgust for the living who flitted among the vampires like flies clinging to dead flesh. Though Sarah did see one human boy leaving just after she came in, most of these humans would stay, out of either ignorance or perverted loyalty.

She didn't like being inside this group without backup, but the short drive between the gas station and this house had only allowed for a few cell-phone calls, which had reached only busy signals and answering machines. She couldn't risk making a serious kill, outnumbered as she was, but if she played nice tonight, she had a good chance of wangling an invitation to the next bash this group hosted. She could bring in the big guns then.

The trick was to avoid being killed—or

munched on. She was posing as free food, human and helpless, but letting a vampire feed on her was further than she was willing to go. Besides, even the weakest vampire would be able to taste the difference between the bland vintage of human blood and the power in her own witch blood.

It was past ten o'clock at night, and the back of Sarah's neck tingled with apprehension. Any hunter worth her blade generally knew better than to stay at a bash after midnight. Called the Devil's Hour, midnight was when the killing was done.

Yet if Sarah wanted an invitation, she needed to stay and convince these creatures she was one of the idiotic humans who bared their throats willingly. Any hunter, from the most amateur to the most respected, would give his right eye and his life for a chance to take down a group of vampires this strong.

Sarah befriended the girl she had followed, and within fifteen minutes she had charmed her way into receiving one of the slick white cards that stated the time and location of the next bash this group was hosting.

Now all she had to do was follow the two

simplest rules any hunter ever learned: Don't get caught, and clean up after yourself.

As the Devil's Hour drew near, Sarah found the weakest of the vampires and made sure she was alone with him when the clock struck.

"I don't think Kaleo meant this room to be open to the public," her companion pointed out, referring to their vampire host. Sarah recognized the name with revulsion. Nikolas was not the only creature in this group the hunters would love to take down.

Hiding her thoughts, she smiled and put a hand on her companion's shoulder, forcing herself to ignore the unpleasant thickness of his aura. "Maybe I just wanted you all to myself," she teased, meeting his black vampiric eyes.

The fiend got the message and leaned closer to her. Sarah ran her fingers through his ash blond hair, and he wrapped a slender hand around the back of her neck, gently urging her forward.

She leaned her head back, knowing where his gaze would travel. He fell for it, as they always did, and as she felt his lips touch her throat, she reacted.

Shoving him back into the wall, she used

his moment of confusion to draw the silver knife from the sheath on her back. Before he could recover his wits, she slammed the blade into his chest, then twisted the knife to make sure his heart was completely destroyed. Vampiric power lived in the blood, and any well-trained hunter knew to twist the knife and obliterate the source of that power. Even Sarah, with a silver blade forged by magic thousands of years old, was still careful. The Vida blade would poison any vampire it scratched, but there was no reason to be careless.

The kill was silent and quick; no one outside even knew this monster was down. Sarah absently wiped her clean hand on her jeans, brushing away the tingling aftereffect of touching him, and touched her throat to reassure herself that there were no puncture marks.

She tucked the body into a corner, knowing this house would probably be abandoned for a while after this bash—that was one of the techniques the vampires used to keep hunters from tracking them down. They were rarely stupid enough to sleep in the same house where they killed.

For a moment she paused, pondering the lifeless body, wondering how any person would willingly become a creature who fed on humanity, a monstrous parasite. He would have taken her blood and killed her had she not killed him first.

She shook her head. It was dead, as it should have been when the vampire blood first froze its heart years ago. That was all that mattered.

Checking herself for blood and finding none, she took a moment to relax as she waited for some time to pass.

She sensed another vampire behind her but forced herself to turn slowly, as if a little groggy. She recognized the vampire immediately. Kaleo had pale blond hair and sculpted features, which would have made him attractive had his aura not been enough to make Sarah's stomach churn. In the midst of his blond features, his black eyes seemed infinitely darker. Kaleo was one of the oldest in his line, and more powerful than any creature Sarah had ever faced.

For a moment, Sarah debated going for her blade. Attacking Kaleo by herself with so many of his kind near would probably mean the end of her life. But it might be worth it.

Before Sarah could make a move, though, Kaleo glanced pointedly to the doorway behind which Sarah had hidden her prey. "What excellent taste," he congratulated her. "He was rather a pain."

A prepared vampire was more difficult to fight than an unsuspecting one. Without hesitation, Sarah went for her knife.

CHAPTER 2

"YOU DROVE HOME LIKE THIS?"

Sarah nodded sharply in answer to the healer's question.

Caryn Smoke shook her head but made no comment.

She was the strongest living member of her line, and had nearly been disowned recently due to her associations with vampires. Sarah had disliked the girl ever since the trial, but Caryn was an effective healer, and Sarah only turned to the best.

Sarah had been raised to ignore pain so it would not incapacitate her in a fight, and tonight those lessons had proved invaluable.

Both bones in her right forearm had broken when Kaleo grabbed her wrist and threw her into a wall; her head had hit hard enough that had she been human it would have knocked her out. Instead, she had simply drawn another knife with her left hand.

Fortunately, Kaleo and his guests had all been more interested in the pleasures willingly provided by their human sycophants than in fighting a vampire hunter, and had quickly lost interest in Sarah and allowed her to escape.

Sarah had been lucky. She had survived because the vampires had gotten bored. That—added to the fact that she hadn't seen Nikolas—grated on her.

It was almost five o'clock in the morning by the time Caryn was finished setting the arm. The healer moved on to deal with Sarah's numerous other scrapes, bruises, and minor sprains when Dominique Vida returned from hunting and came to see her injured daughter. As she sized up Sarah's condition, her expression was calm, but marked with distinct disapproval.

"You were careless," Dominique chastised, after she heard the details of Sarah's

night. "You went into that group unpre-
pared, and you stayed past midnight."

Sarah lowered her gaze, but did not allow
her defiant expression to fall.

Finally Sarah spoke up, her voice sure despite Dominique's reproach. "Nikolas was
there." Dominique could complain all she
liked about Sarah's carelessness, but if Nikolas was part of that group, then they had a
lead to finding him.

"Nikolas?" Dominique's voice was sharp.
"You saw him?"

Sarah shook her head. "One of his prey—
marked."

"That doesn't help much unless you saw
the vampire himself," Dominique pointed
out dryly, and Sarah set her jaw to keep from
arguing. "And now we have no way of tracking him down." Sarah did not bother turning
over the invitation she had received. After
having teased and released the hunter they
had found in their midst, the vampires would
know better than to host the bash she had
mistakenly been invited to.

"You're set," Caryn said, her normally
quiet voice raised to interrupt the conversation. She patted the cast on Sarah's arm gen-

tly. "You'll need a week or so to heal completely, and until then I recommend that you take it easy. Okay?" The last was said with a sharp look to Dominique.

The Vida matriarch nodded. "Thank you for your help, Caryn. Sorry to bother you so late."

Caryn shrugged, her fatigue visible. "No problem. I was in the neighborhood, at a SingleEarth hospital."

Dominique did not react to the remark, and Sarah copied her mother's neutral mask. SingleEarth. The organization was growing by leaps and bounds, with humans, witches, vampires, and shapeshifters joining, all working toward a common cause: unite all the creatures on Earth. Though a noble goal, it was never going to work. Vampires were hunters, evil by nature, and most were incapable of containing their need for bloodshed. Even the vampires at SingleEarth, who survived by feeding on animals or willing donors, admitted that it was painful to live without killing.

"I guess you probably won't be at school tomorrow?" Caryn asked on her way out.

Sarah glanced to her mother, but saw no

sympathy. "I'll be there." No matter how hard a night Sarah had had, Dominique was not one to allow her daughter to slack off, not even for a few days so she could start at her new school on Monday. Sarah would start bright and early on Wednesday morning.

Sarah had been expelled from her last school for fighting on school grounds. In the process of extinguishing a vampire, some school property had been broken, and the administration had not been particularly understanding. Only some quick thinking by Sarah's sister, Adianna, had kept anyone from finding the body.

After the incident, Dominique had decided to move her daughter away from the constant excitement of the city and into a dull Massachusetts suburb named Acton. Caryn and her family lived there.

Dominique returned upstairs to sleep, and Caryn caught Sarah's good arm.

"I should warn you. There are a few vampires in the school." Upon Sarah's look, she added sternly, "They're harmless, and they have every right to be there. If you hurt any of them—"

"If they're harmless, I'll just ignore them. I

can't afford to get kicked out of another school, anyway. Okay?" Sarah offered. Caryn nodded.

Sarah's pride, already ground into the dirt, deflated even more when the door opened again and her sister entered the house.

"Hey, little sis," Adianna greeted her. Noticing the cast, she added, "Rough night?"

Adianna Vida, one year Sarah's senior, was almost as perfect as their mother—intelligent and controlled. She had graduated last year, but was taking a semester off before starting college to train harder, and to "look out for" her little sister.

Right then Adianna's blond hair was tousled, and Sarah saw a smear of blood on her dark blue jeans as if she had wiped a knife clean. She had obviously been fighting, and she had just as obviously won.

Adianna patted her sister's shoulder as she passed toward the stairs. "Rest up. The world will survive without you for a week or so."

CHAPTER 3

SEVEN-THIRTY-FIVE is a beastly hour to begin school, Sarah thought, as she opened her locker. The bell rang and she sighed. Hopefully being the new girl would excuse her tardiness. It certainly had no other perks. She thought fleetingly of the hunting companions she had left behind, with whom she had crashed bashes and stalked the darkest corners of the city. By morning, rarely had a blade been left clean.

She forcibly banished such thoughts. She was here now, and it was time to begin this new life.

Her first block was American history, and

though she located it easily, the class had already begun when she slipped through the door.

"Sarah Green?" the teacher confirmed as Sarah turned over the folded pink pass from the office. Mr. Smith was a balding, tired-looking man whose crisp suit pants and shirt seemed out of place in the high school. He gestured toward the class. "Take a seat . . . there's one open right next to Robert—"

"Actually, someone's sitting there," one of the boys in the back of the room called. As Sarah's attention turned to Robert, she realized that he looked vaguely familiar, but she couldn't place his face in her memory. He had looked up just long enough to see who had come in the door, and was now writing something in a notebook. The desk next to him appeared empty to Sarah; the chair was vacant.

Mr. Smith looked surprised, but he skimmed the class again.

"There's a seat here," someone else called, and Sarah glanced to see who had spoken.

Black hair, fair skin, *black* eyes. Vampire. She recognized him instantly, but Mr. Smith was already hustling her toward the empty seat.

"Christopher Ravena," the leech said, introducing himself as she slid into her chair. He nodded across the class. "That's my sister, Nissa." The girl he had gestured to waved slightly. Though her hair was a shade lighter, the resemblance between the siblings was marked—including the mild vampiric aura.

"Nice to meet you," she answered politely, though inside she grimaced. *This could be a very long year.*

The aura of the vampire beside her was so faint that her skin wasn't even tingling. He was either very young or very weak, and she could tell that he did not feed on human prey. Probably SingleEarth, harmless as Caryn had said. His sister was almost as weak, and although her aura showed a hint of human blood—probably from one of the plethora of humans at SingleEarth willing to bare their throats—it was obvious she did not kill when she hunted. Neither of them would be able to sense Sarah's aura, so unless they knew her by sight, they would likely assume that she was just another human.

Mr. Smith was talking to her again, and she turned her attention back to him. "Sarah, as you'll see, I like to begin class with a conversation about current events, to keep us involved in the present as well as the history." Raising his voice to address all the students, he asked, "Now, who has something to share?"

The number of hands raised—none—was not overly surprising. Most of the students looked like they were still asleep.

"I know it's early," Mr. Smith said, encouragingly, "but you are allowed to wake up any time now. Who heard the news last night? What happened in our world?"

Finally a few hands tiredly rose, but most of the students had better things to do. The girl sitting in front of Sarah was reading a book that looked like it was probably an English assignment. Nearby, another student was doing Spanish homework. The teacher was either oblivious, or he just didn't care. The news story that was being repeated by a girl in the first row wasn't all that fascinating, anyway.

"Did you just move in?" Christopher asked, his voice quiet to avoid the teacher's attention. He had a slight accent—not quite a drawl, but smooth and unhurried, with a hint of the South.

Sarah nodded, trying to keep a small portion of her attention focused on the dull classroom conversation, while keeping the rest on the two vampires. "My mother got a new job, teaching in the next town." It was a plausible lie, which she had come up with earlier.

Mr. Smith moved back in time to the Civil War, and Sarah took notes furiously for an excuse to avoid Christopher's attempts at conversation. The class was dull, and she already knew most of the information, but if she made a good impression now, Mr. Smith was more likely to cut her some slack later.

Christopher's silence lasted only until the bell. "How'd you hurt your arm?" he asked as Sarah awkwardly shuffled papers into her backpack after class.

"Thrown off a horse," Sarah lied effortlessly. "She's usually a sweet creature, but something spooked her." As she lifted the heavy backpack, she wondered how in the world humans could possibly carry these things around all day. Her witch blood made

Sarah stronger than an average human—her five-foot-four, 130-pound body could bench-press 300 pounds—but she wondered how the humans managed.

"Do you need help with that?" Christopher offered, gesturing to the bag. "What class do you have next?"

"Chemistry," she answered. "I can handle it."

"I didn't mean to suggest you couldn't," Christopher responded smoothly. "You just shouldn't have to bother. I've got biology next, anyway, so our classes are near each other."

She examined his expression, but he appeared sincere. For whatever his reasons, he was honestly trying to play the part of a human teenage boy—an unusually polite one, but human nevertheless.

She didn't want to make a scene, so she surrendered her backpack, and Christopher carried it without effort, which did not surprise her. If she could lift 300 pounds, as a weak vampire he could probably bench-press a ten-wheeler with about as much effort.

"Thanks," she forced out, glad the words sounded sincere.

Though her chemistry class was blessedly human, Christopher's sister was in sculpture with Sarah for the third block of the day.

Sarah's skills with clay were minimal; she had signed up for this class mainly so she could do something low stress without homework. She'd be lucky if she could make a ball. Nissa, on the other hand, had a great deal of talent, which helped Sarah place her in a way that the girl's weak aura had not: Kendra's line.

Kendra was the fourth fledgling of Siete, creator of all the vampires. Though Sarah had never met her, the woman was rumored to be stunning in form and fierce in temper. She was a lover of all the arts, as were almost all of her descendents. Kaleo, with whom Sarah had had her uncomfortable run-in the night before, was Kendra's first fledgling.

All these thoughts passed through Sarah's mind quickly as she watched Nissa craft a young man's figure in the soft clay, humming quietly to herself as she worked. He sat upon a rustic bench, a violin perched on his shoulder. The bow was a fine coil of clay supported by a piece of wire at its neck.

Nissa looked up from her work and noticed Sarah watching.

"That's really impressive," Sarah offered, surprised to find her words completely sincere.

"Thanks." Nissa smiled, looking back at the form. "But I can't get the face quite right." She indicated the shapeless globe where the features should be, surrounded by carefully etched hair.

"Better than mine."

Nissa laughed lightly. "Considering you just started today and you're only working with your left hand, it's not bad."

The vampire carefully wrapped her figure in plastic so it would not dry, and then shifted over to offer suggestions on Sarah's project, which was a sickly-looking clay dog. They worked together for the last ten minutes of class, during which Sarah almost forgot what she was talking to.

"You could put a wire in his tail so it wouldn't fall like that. What kind of dog is it?" Nissa asked.

Sarah shrugged. "I don't really know.

My mother doesn't like dogs, so I've never had one."

In fact, Dominique hated dogs. She was very against animals and witches mixing; the Vida line was one of the few that had never used familiars in its magic.

"It could kind of look like a Lab, if you squared off the nose," the girl suggested. Under Nissa's expert assistance the smooth white clay turned into an almost-recognizable animal.

"What do you have next?" Nissa asked as they packed the dog in plastic.

"Lunch, I think."

"Great! You're with Christopher and me." The girl's exuberance was infectious, but still Sarah hesitated at Nissa's implied invitation. She could be sociable during class, but there were pages of laws in the Vida books detailing how far any relations with vampires could go. While the school cafeteria was not mentioned by name, Sarah was pretty sure it would be considered unnecessary association.

Still, Nissa walked with her through the halls, and even followed Sarah to her locker when she tried to use it as an excuse to drop the vampire.

Inside the locker, on the top shelf, Sarah noticed something she had not put there: a white piece of paper, on which a profile had been drawn carefully in pencil. She immediately recognized the figure as herself; her hair spilled over her shoulders and onto the desk as she wrote.

Nissa just shrugged when she saw the drawing and gave an understanding smile as Sarah read the initials signed in light script in the bottom corner. *CR.* It was from Christopher; he had probably drawn it while sitting right next to her in history class, when Sarah had been trying to ignore him.

CHAPTER 4

NISSA LED THE WAY to the table where she and her brother usually sat; Christopher was already there. Sarah thought again how lucky it was that neither Christopher nor Nissa was strong enough to read her aura.

Lucky . . . yeah, right. If she had been lucky, they would have recognized her and avoided her from the start. As it was, she was going to need to find some way to break off the friendship they were obviously attempting to form—preferably without broadcasting her heritage to two vampires she knew next to nothing about.

"Sarah, sit down," Christopher called. "How was sculpture?"

"Much more interesting than Mr. Smith's history lecture," Sarah answered vaguely. She hesitated by the table's side, but as Nissa tossed her backpack on one of the chairs, Sarah reluctantly grabbed a seat of her own.

"Hey, Nissa . . ." A human boy approached Nissa, but hesitated when he saw Sarah. She recognized him as Robert, the boy from her first class. The look he directed at her was anything but friendly. He turned back to Nissa. "I was wondering . . . if you're going to the dance this weekend."

Nissa looked from Robert to Sarah. "I'm going stag."

"Oh, um . . ." He paused, then said something hurriedly that might have been, "See you there," before he slipped back into the mass of students.

"What was that about?" Nissa asked as soon as the boy was gone. "Did you kill the boy's baby sister or something? Robert usually goes after anything with legs," she joked.

"I never met him before today," Sarah

answered honestly, watching his sandy brown hair bob through the crowd.

Christopher shrugged. "Don't worry, you're not missing much," he said lightly. "Robert has been hitting on Nissa ever since he first saw her, and he's a royal pain."

Sarah did not brush off the interaction as lightly as Christopher and Nissa, but she did allow them to change the subject, while her mind stayed focused on the incident.

Sarah was of average human height, and well shaped from a high metabolism and a vigorous exercise routine. Her fair blond hair was long, with enough body that it fell down her back in soft waves, and her sapphire eyes were stunning. To top it off, her aura was powerfully charismatic, and humans were drawn to it. Though she had heard about humans who were naturally anxious around vampires and humanity's other predators, that was obviously not the case with Robert; and while Sarah had received numerous phone numbers from strange boys, she had *never* met one who instinctively disliked her.

The only possibility she could think of was that Robert was somehow bonded to the vampires. Sarah would have sensed a blood bond, but maybe . . . the thought trailed off with disgust. There were humans who were addicted to vampires. They didn't need to be blood bonded to one monster; they gave their blood willingly to any who would take it. Enough contact with the leeches, and he could have formed the same kind of instinctual aversion to witches that most humans had for strong vampires.

"Sarah?" Christopher's voice pulled her back to the real world. In her mind she played back the conversation she had missed.

"Yeah, sure." Then, "Wait, no. I can't."

They had asked if she was going to go to the dance the school was hosting on Saturday—the Halloween dance, which, according to Nissa, was the only school dance worth going to until the senior prom in the spring.

"Why not?" Christopher asked, obviously disappointed.

Nissa added, "If you're worried about getting a costume, I'm sure we could find something for you, and they sell the tickets at the door."

"No, it's not that. It's just . . . I've got family coming over that weekend, and my mother would never let me go out."

"Shame," Christopher sighed, slightly wistful. "Nice family, or wish-you-could-lose-them family?"

Actually, the "family" included many of the local witches—the rest of the Vida line, some of Caryn Smoke's kin, and a few young men from the Marinitch line. Even human Wiccans celebrated Samhain, and for Sarah's kind, it was one of the few holidays still left that they could celebrate without unnerving the human world. Dominique Vida hosted a circle on October 31 every year, open to every descendant of Macht—the immortal mother of Sarah's kind.

"Some nice, some barely tolerable," Sarah answered, thinking of the Smoke witches in the second group. The peaceful healers had a tendency to preach about peace and unity— an idea that would have been tolerable, had it not included vampires. Luckily, Caryn herself, along with many of the most offensive give-peace-a-chance callers, would celebrate at SingleEarth instead of spending the holiday with hunters.

Yet even as she thought with contempt of Caryn's association with vampires, here she was speaking with two leeches who might or might not belong to the painfully overgrown SingleEarth.

She had to end this. *Some tolerant association is necessary to preserve human safety and forbearance, but friendship and love with such creatures as you hunt is impossible, dangerous, abhorrent, and as such, forbidden.* She could quote the Vida laws back to front, and that line stood out in bold in her memory. Going beyond the bonds of what was necessary to keep her cover in school could at best stain her reputation; other hunters would not trust someone who had befriended the monsters. At worst, Dominique could call her to trial, and that would be a disaster.

"I've got to go," Sarah said abruptly.

The two vampires seemed startled, but they did not try to stop her. "See you later," Christopher said amiably.

"Yeah . . . maybe." She hoped not.

She ducked out of the cafeteria and swung into the girls' bathroom, shuddering as she caught sight of herself in the mirror. What had she thought she was doing? She had dropped her guard around them. Already she thought about the pair with some affection—they were Christopher and Nissa, not two leeches she might one day have to kill.

That was dangerous. Knowing your prey can cause hesitation, and when one is a vampire hunter, hesitation ends in death.

Sarah managed to avoid them for the rest of the day. She had calculus with Christopher, but the only free seat was across the room from him, and for that she was grateful. She needed some time to decide on how she would deal with them before she had another chance to talk to them.

CHAPTER 5

SARAH SLEPT POORLY that night. With her broken arm, she felt like a caged leopard with too much energy and nothing to use it on. It was nearly three o'clock when she finally drifted into sleep, and even then she was restless, plagued by nightmares.

By the time she got to school, she felt less like a leopard and more like a slug. It was a pity that human drugs were neutralized by her system upon absorption, because she could have used some serious caffeine.

It took her two tries to get the combination to her locker right, and as she tossed in her coat, she managed to knock something down from the top shelf.

The vase shattered upon impact with the dirty school floor, scattering water, glass, and three white roses. The sound of breaking glass drove a shiver up Sarah's spine, bringing back all too vividly her dream from the night before.

Memories of her father's death often haunted her sleep. Though she had tried to forget that day, to perfect her control the way Dominique and Adianna had, she wasn't strong enough, and she never had been.

At seven years old, she had stumbled across her father's body on the front step of the house. The vampires had caught the hunter and kept him for weeks, bleeding him a little each day. Bloody kisses marked his arms where the leeches had cut into his skin so they could lick the blood away.

Adianna had dealt with the news calmly, as had Dominique. Every hunter knew how dangerous his life was, and was prepared for death. But Sarah had been so young, and when she had stumbled over the cold body of her father, when his blood had coated her hand, she had lost control.

She had hit a window, demolishing it pane by pane until Dominique had dragged her away, horrified not by her husband's death, but by her daughter's reaction.

The death had become a lesson. Dominique had bound Sarah's powers for a week afterward, both as a punishment and to teach her how to deal with pain. She had healed as slowly as a human, from three broken fingers and numerous lacerations on her hand and arm. In the meantime Dominique had her train with the older hunters, fighting until her hand throbbed and every muscle ached. Though binding her magic could not take away the years of training, her reflexes, or even most of her strength, the loss had left her shaken and her abilities meaningless. That weakness had terrified her ever since.

Shuddering from the memory, Sarah dragged herself back to the present. Ignoring the glass, she carefully picked up the roses and the card that had been tied to the vase with a white ribbon.

The white blooms were beautiful, perfect, with the sweet scent that so many long-stemmed roses lacked. A picture done in professional charcoal accompanied them—a pair of eyes framed with the pale lashes Sarah saw every time she looked into a mirror.

She read the poem at least ten times before she even reached class, and finally resolved to speak to Christopher.

> *Blue like sapphire beneath a morning sun,*
> *Burning with fire of a crystalline soul.*
> *A laughter that never quite reaches inside,*
> *Where secrets weather like untouched gold.*

The words were beautiful—and truer than Christopher realized. If he had known even the slightest of Sarah's secrets, he would never have spoken to her in the first place.

She had steeled herself to talk to him by the time she reached her history class, only to have Mr. Smith immediately divide them into groups for a project. Her group included two humans she had not met before, and the mysterious Robert, who was not hiding his hostility any better today.

"What's eating *you*?" one of their other group members demanded after he shot down yet another of their ideas. "If you don't want to help, then just keep your mouth shut. Don't make *your* bad day *mine*."

By the time the class was over Sarah was glad to get away from Robert—the human had been putting out waves of contempt and distrust strong enough that they were making her stomach churn. She would need to speak to him sometime soon, but not here, not in front of other humans.

She had calmed down slightly by sculpture, where she continued to work on the sickly dog Nissa had named Splotch. Nissa finished her figure. Under her expert hands, the violinist gained clear Roman features, sympathetic eyes, and wicked, sensual lips.

"Someone you know?" Sarah asked. The face was so vivid, so alive, she felt like she should recognize it.

Nissa nodded, pausing in her work. "Yeah." Her voice was soft, sad.

"Who is he?"

"A . . ." She trailed off, as if none of the words she had been thinking of would work. "Someone I used to love. His name is Kaleo."

Sarah's heart skipped as she heard the name. Kaleo had a reputation for ruining lives on a whim, and changing young women into vampires whom he fancied himself in love with.

If Nissa was one of Kaleo's fledglings, Sarah had to pity the girl.

"Anyway, it's over," Nissa stated. "I miss him sometimes, but . . . it's over."

"Then why are you sculpting him?" The question was sharper than Sarah meant it to be.

"He is beautiful," the girl said wistfully. Then she jumped as the bell rang for lunch.

They did not speak as they cleaned up their stations, and Nissa stayed behind to talk to the teacher while Sarah swung by her locker. Inside she found another present from Christopher—a picture of her left hand, which she had been writing with since she had broken her right arm.

Her nails were cut short so they wouldn't hinder her grip on her knife; there was a small scar on the back from the glass window she had punched the day her father had been killed. It looked like a pale teardrop.

On the back of the drawing was another poem.

Skin like ivory, perfect; A goddess, she must be.

*Slender fingers, unadorned; beautiful
    simplicity.
A single teardrop; when did it fall?
Could this goddess be mortal, after all?*

If only he knew, Sarah thought dryly. That scar was left over from the least perfect moment of her life.

Yet somehow Christopher had made the flaw beautiful, no longer a badge of her dishonor, but a mystery for an artist to unravel.

CHAPTER 6

"CHRISTOPHER ... are these from you?"
she asked at lunch, careful to make her tone
light as she placed the two picture-poems on
the table. Christopher's eyes fell to them, and
he smiled.

"Yes."

He didn't ask if she liked them, and he
didn't seem embarrassed.

Sarah was flattered, and somewhat surprised by Christopher's easy confidence. Even
so, her natural suspicion surfaced. "Why?"

"Because," he answered seriously, "you
make a good subject. Your hair, for one, is

like a shimmering waterfall. It's so fair that it catches the light. It makes you seem like you have a halo about you. And your eyes — they're such a pure color, not washed out at all, deep as the ocean. And your expression . . . intense and yet somehow detached, as if you see more of the world than the rest of us."

Flustered, she could think of no way to respond. Did he just say this stuff from the top of his head? Only her strict Vida control kept her from blushing.

Meanwhile Nissa entered the cafeteria. She started to sit, then glanced from the pictures, to Christopher, to Sarah. "Should I go somewhere else?"

Christopher nodded to a chair, answering easily, "Sit down. We aren't exchanging dark secrets — yet."

Nissa flashed a teasing look to her brother as she took a seat. "As his sister, I feel the need to inform you, Sarah, that Christopher has been talking about you incessantly."

Christopher smiled, unembarrassed. "I suppose I might have been."

"Especially your eyes — he never shuts up

about your eyes," Nissa confided, and this time Christopher shrugged.

"They're beautiful," he said casually. "Beauty should be looked at, not ignored. I try to capture it on paper, but that's really impossible with eyes, because they have a life no still portrait can capture."

Sarah's voice was tied up so tightly she thought she might be able to speak again sometime next year. No one had ever talked about her—or to her—with such admiration.

Luckily, Nissa changed the subject. "Christopher is an incredible artist, but he refuses to take classes."

Christopher laughed, shaking his head. "I draw when I see something I need to draw; I can't draw on command. Nissa convinced me to try an art class once, and I failed it."

They talked casually for the rest of lunch. Sarah found herself relaxing in their company as they told jokes and teased one another good-naturedly. Visions of shattered glass faded from her mind, replaced by light banter. This was easy; these people were kind. What could be evil in their friendship?

"Sarah?" The voice just behind her left shoulder was questioning, a bit sharp.

"Adianna." The muscles in Sarah's neck clenched so tightly she felt like they would tear when she turned her head.

"Can I talk to you?" Adianna's tone was pleasant, so it wouldn't make the vampires suspicious, but the expression that glittered in her eyes was dangerous.

"I'll be right back." Sarah gathered her backpack, leaving the two pictures on the table so as not to draw Adianna's attention to them, and followed the other witch into the hall.

"What was going on there?"

"They're in a few of my classes," Sarah answered, forcing herself to be calm despite the fact that she felt like she was on trial during the Spanish Inquisition. "They're perfectly harmless."

"To humans maybe," Adianna answered instantly. "Not to our kind. What if Mother found out? You honestly think she would see them as 'harmless'?"

"She won't find out," Sarah snapped, softly. "Could we have this conversation outside? If they try, they'll be able to hear us here."

Adianna nodded and remained silent until

they reached the hill outside the school. "Sarah . . ." She sighed. "What are you try- ing to do to yourself? Mother would throw a fit if she knew you were hanging out with their kind. Even I can barely stand the thought of it."

"Dominique doesn't need to know every- thing I do during my life—"

"Sarah!" Adianna's voice was sharp, but Sarah knew it was more due to surprise and worry than censure. "I don't understand why you would even want to spend your time with them, much less break Vida law to do so. As for what Mother does and doesn't need to know—Dominique is the one who decides what information is her business, and you well know what she would think about your having vampiric friends."

"Are you going to tell her?" Sarah's voice was soft, cool. She couldn't stop Adianna if she insisted on going to Dominique, but she made it very clear by her tone that she would not easily forgive the betrayal.

"Sarah, I understand what you're going through." There was obvious effort behind Adianna's even tone. "I've been there. You aren't one of the humans. You don't have any friends here. You just lost some of your oldest hunting partners by moving here, and faced one of the closest encounters you have ever had with death. It's understandable that you have doubts."

"I have no doubts." Sarah had to take a breath to control herself before she continued. "They don't know what I am—they think I'm human. They aren't a threat." After a pause she decided to speak the truth. "Haven't you ever once wanted someone you could talk to about something besides killing? Someone who has no idea about your power and is simply a friend? It's really nice, Adianna. To have someone treat me like a human girl instead of like a killer is really, *really* nice. What's even better is that I don't have to worry every night whether some screwup of mine just got them killed. I don't have to watch my back every moment—"

"That is exactly why the law says you can't befriend them," Adianna interrupted. "Because you relax your guard. They are *killers*, Sarah. I don't care if they don't kill now, or even if they never touch a human and survive on animal blood. They kill by nature, and eventually that nature will destroy whatever shreds of humanity they may have left. If at that time they are still your 'friends,' it will simply mean you are handy for a snack."

Adianna paused to collect herself, then added more softly, "I don't want to lose you, Sarah. I don't want you getting killed by these two when they turn on you—and note I say when, not if. But worse, I don't want you getting killed for these two. Do you really care so much for them that you will risk getting yourself disowned?"

"Adianna—"

Adianna shook her head, looking tired. "I can't physically stop you from talking to them, but I won't let you get yourself killed for a leech's friendship," she stated clearly. "I won't tell Mother what I've seen so far, but if you three get any closer, I will, while there's still a chance that she'll let you off with a warning." She turned to leave, then added, "And, Sarah? If they ever get you hurt, whether they do it directly or it's because

Dominique finds out you have been talking to them, I will kill them myself."

Sarah wanted to respond with anger, but thought better of it. Adianna was letting her off easy, so she just nodded.

"If you care about them like you claim to, leave your new friends alone," Adianna suggested in a rare show of compassion. "Remember them fondly if you care to, but let go of them, or you'll all end up dead."

Adianna glanced back toward the school. "I'm sorry to have to threaten you, Sarah. That wasn't what I came here for."

"I figured."

"I came to tell you that Dominique is flying off this afternoon to train a group of amateur hunters, and I've just received a call to deal with some leeches up in Chicago. We should both be back in time for the holiday." Sarah took in the news without surprise. If it had not been for Adianna's attempts to keep her little sister informed, Sarah would probably never know where her family was. "You'll be fine here?" Though phrased like a question, the last line was a statement. Sarah had spent plenty of time home alone when

Adianna and Dominique were off on their various missions.

"Be careful," Sarah told her sister.

Adianna answered seriously, "You too."

They separated, Sarah going back inside the school, and Adianna toward the parking lot.

The bell had rung while Sarah had been speaking with Adianna, so she went immediately to her class, arriving late. Luckily, the teacher was tolerant because she was new to the school; Sarah was in no mood for a detention tonight. She had too much on her mind.

What was she going to do about Christopher and Nissa?

Adianna's worries were legitimate—at least the ones involving Mother and Vida law. If Dominique found out about her budding friendship with two vampires, she would kill them.

Sarah flexed her hand. Old phantom pain reminded her of the other danger. Sarah had had her powers bound once; she could not imagine what it would be like to have them stripped forever.

Sarah almost convinced herself to give up her new friends, for their safety as well as her own. She managed to avoid Christopher's questioning looks in calculus that afternoon, and she said nothing but a casual greeting in response to his hello after class.

Christopher had to stay after to talk to the teacher, and Sarah managed to slip out before he was free. She was home, sitting on her bed, before she found his next gift tucked into her calculus notebook; she had no idea when he had managed to slip it there.

It was another drawing—her, dressed in a pale gown. Above her outstretched left hand, the sun and the moon were suspended; she held the earth in her right hand. A sash was tied about her waist, embroidered with stars. In elegant script, a poem had been written down the page on the figure's left side.

> *Fantasy, a shining goddess,*
> *She controls the tides.*
> *Fantasy, a brilliant goddess.*
> *She controls our lives.*
>
> *Fantasy, a golden goddess —*
> *In her hands is the light.*
> *Fantasy, a silver goddess —*
> *In her hands is the night.*

———

Sarah got up and tucked the card into her desk. Next time she saw Christopher she would tell him the truth—about her family, and about all the laws she was breaking. She would tell him the truth, and he would be able to leave her alone without getting hurt.

CHAPTER 7

"SARAH, IS SOMETHING WRONG?" Nissa asked the next day during sculpture. "Christopher told me you were avoiding him yesterday afternoon . . . he was sure he had done something to offend you."

Christopher? Offend? She doubted he was capable of such a thing.

Sarah grasped at, and then lost, a handy lie. "Look, I . . . it's nothing really, okay?" Sarah said awkwardly. "I can't really explain."

"That's fine." Nissa's voice was soft, understanding. "If it's none of my business, I'm not going to be a pain. But don't just ditch

Christopher—he's a nice guy, and he deserves an explanation if you're not interested."

By the time Sarah saw Christopher at lunch, her resolve to break off the friendship had wavered. He greeted her with a smile and a hello, not asking about her efforts to ignore him the day before.

"Hey, I'm sorry about yesterday—"

"No big deal," Christopher answered easily. "I was kind of worried about you, but . . . well, if you're talking to me again today, it can't have been anything too awful."

"I'm sorry anyway." But his light words and easy confidence made Sarah smile again. "Christopher—"

"Look, we've got to duck out soon to meet with our partners about that history project," Nissa apologized before Sarah could finish her sentence. "Are you sure you aren't going to the Halloween dance this weekend, Sarah? It'll be a lot of fun."

Sarah shook her head. Dominique would throw a fit if she missed the holiday celebrations. "I really can't." She debated asking them to meet up with her after the project, somewhere private where she could tell them and be done with it, but they were already on their way out before she could make up her mind.

Christopher touched Sarah's shoulder as he walked by, a casual gesture that nevertheless made her flinch; physical contact with a vampire made her skin crawl, no matter how weak he was. If he noticed the withdrawal, Christopher did not react to it.

"Catch you later."

"Yeah."

A test kept them from talking in that afternoon's calculus class, but Christopher caught Sarah afterward.

"How'd it go?"

The vampire rolled his eyes skyward. "Math is not my thing." Changing the subject, he said, "I've got to run to a drama club meeting, so I can't talk long now, but . . . well, since you can't go to the dance, I was wondering if you might want to go for lunch on Saturday."

"I don't know." She *did* know, actually, and the answer was "Absolutely not." Spending time with vampires at school, where she had little else to do, was one thing; spending time with them otherwise, when she could be training or hunting, was twisting the laws further than even she could rationalize.

"Give me a call sometime, okay?" He jotted down his phone number on a piece of scrap paper, and then hurried away to his meeting.

Sarah skimmed the paper after Christopher left, and tucked it into her pocket.

Nine o'clock that evening found Sarah on the phone, trying without success to get through to Christopher or Nissa. Nissa was right—they both deserved more than to get a simple brush-off. She had decided to call, arrange a time when they could talk, and tell them everything.

Beep . . . beep . . . beep . . .

The sickly B-flat of the busy signal sliced through her yet again, as it had every time she had heard it over the last two hours.

She hung up the phone with a sigh, and pulled out the local yellow pages to find the Ravenas' address. Her mind was made up, and she didn't want to risk chickening out again. She patted the coat's pocket to make sure her keys were in place, and instinctively checked for the knife on her back—a hunter never went anywhere without it—then slipped out to her car.

As she drove, she found herself hoping wildly that Christopher and Nissa would tell her they were part of SingleEarth. If they were, then even Dominique could not forbid Sarah to associate with them—it would be an insult against the witches who ran that organization. Dominique would be furious at her daughter, but she couldn't kill them, or disown Sarah.

Considering how weak they both are, they're probably part of SingleEarth, Sarah tried to reassure herself. *Please, let them be in SingleEarth.*

She jumped, swerving, as a squirrel darted in front of her car. *Calm down, Sarah. Focus.*

Try as she might, her strict control was shattered. She had been purely scatterbrained all evening, and was grateful that she wasn't expecting a fight tonight.

As she parked in Christopher and Nissa's driveway, she thought she heard faint music from the house, but it might have been her imagination. Bracing herself, she knocked on the door.

CHAPTER 8

SOMEONE SARAH DID NOT KNOW opened the door. Black eyes gave him away as a vampire, but his light aura showed him to be almost as weak as Nissa.

"Come on in," the vampire greeted her. Sarah could only nod mutely as she realized what was going on. She had just walked in on a bash.

"Thanks," she answered, dazed. The vampire gave her a strange look, but Sarah paid no heed to him, because her attention had just been drawn to a couple seated on the couch.

A more naïve guest might assume they

were making out. One pale hand was wrapped around the back of the boy's neck, and the girl's long hair fell around her face, blocking from view the seam between her lips and the human boy's throat. His eyes were half closed, and one hand twined absently in the vampire's hair, holding her to his throat.

Sarah recognized the dark hair, the slender form, and she wished she did not. Nissa.

Forcing her attention to the rest of the room, her aura brushing over the others, Sarah picked out the vampires easily. This crowd was weak, not killers—and for that she thanked every god and goddess she had ever heard of—but she did not recognize any of them from SingleEarth, either.

That meant there was some danger here for her. Even vampires who did not frequently kill would be nervous in the presence of a Vida, and entering a large group of them, barely armed and weakened by injury, seemed a bad idea.

She was about to leave, but the vampire who had opened the door was talking again. "I haven't seen you around here before," he said. "Who invited you?" Though his tone was not exactly suspicious, she could tell the vampire was uneasy around her. Having someone ask about her was unusual; at most of the bashes she had crashed, the vampires didn't care who a guest was, so long as she could bleed.

"She's with me." Sarah turned, barely checking her instinct to draw her knife, as she sensed someone approach behind her.

The vampire who had been asking sighed. "I should have known." He wandered off.

Christopher ran his hands through his short black hair, nervous. "Sarah . . . I would have invited you, but . . ." She could guess his thoughts. *How do you explain something like this to someone you assume is human?*

"You don't have to explain," Sarah offered in an attempt to save the vampire the unease of beginning the conversation. She could sense Christopher's shock even through his midnight eyes.

"I don't?"

Out of the corner of her eye, Sarah saw Nissa release the human she had been feeding on. He lay back, a bit dazed, but he looked like he would be fine; if there was anything a vampire knew, it was how much blood a human could afford to lose without being harmed.

The girl looked up, and her eyes widened as she saw Sarah standing with Christopher. She wiped her lips clear of blood with the back of her hand.

"I already know what you are." The sentence had been directed at Christopher, though Sarah was busy reading Nissa's features. Seeing blood on her friend's mouth had unnerved her.

"Why don't we go upstairs for a minute?" Christopher suggested, looking from his sister to his unexpected guest. Nissa nodded.

"That sounds good," Sarah answered. Christopher led the way, and Sarah saw Nissa quickly snatch a mint from a table next to the couch before the wall cut her off from view.

A few moments later, the three gathered in Nissa's room, which was not open to guests. Sarah hesitated in the doorway as Nissa and Christopher made themselves comfortable.

The room was surprisingly normal. While Sarah had known better than to expect a coffin, bats, and bricked-over windows, it was still surprising to see the scattering of schoolbooks that littered the desk. A composition book had been tossed casually in a corner amidst a flurry of crumpled paper and pens, and the pastel blue walls were decorated with posters from musicals like *Rent, Les Misérables,* and *West Side Story.*

"Well, then," Nissa breathed, and Sarah caught the scent of mint barely disguising the reek of fresh blood.

Sarah meant to speak instantly, telling them who she was, but Christopher forestalled it, asking hesitantly, "Are you part of SingleEarth? Or . . ."

She barely managed not to laugh at that question. Sarah Vida, a member of SingleEarth? Oh, Dominique would have a heart attack at the very suggestion.

Nevertheless, she was here, talking with two vampires, two *friends* who just happened to be bloodsucking fiends.

She was flattered at least that he thought of SingleEarth before the alternatives. He still thought she was human, and if she was tolerant of his kind, then it stood to reason that she was either part of SingleEarth, or one of those pathetic creatures who chased after the vampires in order to have her blood taken.

"No, I'm not," she said slowly, trying to decide how best to tell the truth. She would rather have been somewhere else, anywhere but in the middle of a house full of vampires she did not know and whose behavior she could not predict. "I didn't know you had a circuit," she stalled.

"It's Nissa's," Christopher answered, nodding to his sister. "She hosts. I just hang out."

The vampire bashes that Sarah frequently crashed followed a pattern. The members of each party circuit alternated hosting, so as to keep the hunters guessing where the next one would be. All that Sarah had attended had been violent, deadly for any humans who attended, but she had heard about ones like this, where the human guests were simply that—guests, not a main course. They donated blood occasionally, but not at risk to their lives.

"Do you go to bashes often?" Nissa asked from her perch on the bed.

"When I can," Sarah answered truthfully, wondering how—and if—she should ease into the topic she had come to discuss. The presence of several unknown vampires downstairs made her a little hesitant to reveal herself.

Christopher flinched, worry in his eyes. "Not all of them are as safe as Nissa's group."

"I know."

"The worst is Kendra's circuit," Nissa warned. "If you stumble on one of theirs, they'll probably kill you without a thought." Softly, she added, "That's the one Kaleo travels in." The name seemed to strike a chord in both vampires, and Sarah remembered Nissa's sculpture of the leech.

Stop stalling, Sarah, she ordered herself, even as she commented, "You were telling me about Kaleo in sculpture."

"Kaleo . . . was the one who changed me," Nissa said hesitantly. She glanced at her brother, who just shrugged.

"If you want to tell it, it's your story," he pointed out.

"We grew up in the South, just before the Civil War," Nissa began softly. "Our father worked at a nearby plantation and I took care of the owner's two daughters, while my brothes worked as stable hands for one of the other wealthy families. We weren't rich, but we were happy. My mother died when Christopher and his twin brother were both very young, and I more or less raised them."

With a sigh, she continued, "We were an artistic family. I was the singer, though both of my brothers had talent in that area too. Christopher would write songs and poetry. Even when he said grace at night, his words could bring you to tears.

"That's what damned us—music and art," Nissa went on. "Because it drew Kaleo to me. He was also an artist. If he hadn't learned about my talent, he never would have given me more than a passing glance. As it was, he fell in love with me . . . and I with him." That admission sounded painful. "I was seventeen, a romantic and an optimist, and Kaleo was—*is*—very handsome, and very charming, especially when he has it in his mind to win someone over." Nissa paused in her story.

When she continued, her voice was barely more than a whisper. "For a while our relationship was wonderful, but I learned what he was when I caught him feeding on the woman I worked for." With difficulty, Nissa explained, "He did not have time to hurt her before I interrupted. She woke up later, unharmed, and I stupidly assumed that Kaleo wasn't dangerous, that he would not have hurt her even if I had not interfered."

Her voice wavered as she confessed, "I forgave him, and even came to love him more. Then he offered me immortality, and I said no." Nissa took a deep breath to keep herself composed. A hint of anger entered her voice, overlaid with sorrow.

"I thought for a while that we could continue as before, but Kaleo doesn't take no for an answer. Eventually he became so insistent that we argued every time we were together, and finally I told him to leave me alone." A moment of silence passed before she continued. "My brothers were twelve and I was barely nineteen when Kaleo killed our father. I could have stopped him, had I been home a minute earlier, but instead I ran in moments after he died. Christopher's twin was there, and he saw everything. Kaleo made it very clear that he would not hesitate to snap my brother's neck if I refused again.

"So I agreed." The words seemed to catch, as Nissa choked back the memory. "I stayed with my brothers for a few years, but my kind does not exist easily in the human world. There was . . . an incident. I changed my brother, and he changed Christopher the next night. And now we're here."

"What happened to your other brother?" Sarah asked. The instant the words were out of her mouth, Christopher's expression made her regret the question.

"He doesn't run with us," Nissa answered quietly. It was clear she didn't want to go into the topic, and Sarah decided not to press.

The silence hung heavy, both vampires obviously contemplating their painful history. Sarah's mind drifted back to her purpose here, but she couldn't tell them now. Not when they had just opened their hearts to her. She couldn't betray a trust like that, even if she hadn't asked for it.

No one seemed to know exactly how to get over the conversation, so Sarah got up and walked around the room a bit. Once again she noticed the school textbooks.

"Why do you go to school?" she asked. "If you're . . . that old, then why bother?" She did not want to do the math to figure out exactly how old.

"If you spend too much time away from humans, you forget your own humanity," Nissa said, her voice distant. "It gets harder to remember that you used to be one of them, and easier to think of them like ... cattle," she finished apologetically. "Most of our kind is like that. They don't see anything wrong with killing humans. Christopher and I decided we needed a reminder." Sarah remembered with unease Adianna's comment about the vampire blood slowly destroying the last shreds of humanity, and was glad she was not immediately called on to speak. Nissa continued with what sounded like forced brightness, "It's nice to actually be part of the human world for a bit, though I suppose I could imagine places more glamorous than high school." With a brief glance to some flyer on her desk, she added, "Speaking of, are you sure you won't come to the Halloween dance? It will be a lot of fun."

Sarah started to argue, but instead just shrugged. *What the hell,* she thought, *I can do this one last thing, can't I?* Dominique would be furious, but the dance would be over early enough for her to make the ceremony at midnight. As Nissa had said, sometimes it was nice to just be a part of the human crowd for a while.

She heard herself answer, "Sure. I'll find a way to come."

CHAPTER 9

SATURDAY NIGHT, Sarah wrote a note to Dominique: *I am going to attend a dance at school, but will be back in plenty of time for the ceremony. Sarah.*

She dressed carefully, added a hint of makeup, and pinned the sleeves of her dress to hide the spring-loaded knife sheath on her left wrist. She could trigger the mechanism with a small burst of power if necessary. Another knife was on her back. She trusted Christopher and Nissa, but no vampire hunter went out unarmed, especially at this time of year. The moon was full, it was the witches' New Year, and her aura flickered around her, strong and bright. She had too many enemies in the vampire world that would be able to recognize it.

Sarah met up with Christopher and Nissa just outside the door to the school.

"Sarah, you look great!" Nissa exclaimed.

Nissa's full skirts billowed around her as she crossed the floor. She was dressed in an emerald-colored Renaissance-style gown that laced up in back and showed off her perfect figure. Christopher had dressed as a Gypsy, with a colorful vest and a multi-colored scarf pulled around his waist.

Sarah was wearing the same dress she would wear for the ceremony later, a light, silvery cotton gown that flowed around her legs when she moved. Around her waist, in place of the silver belt she would wear at midnight, was a sapphire sash that matched her eyes. It was embroidered with silver stars, and had been hidden somewhere in the back of her closet. She had not worn it in a very long time; it had been a gift from her sister, before Adianna had given up such frivolous things like sisterly teasing and birthday presents in order to follow in Dominique's emotionless footsteps.

The constellations on the barely worn sash reminded Sarah of the picture Christopher had drawn. Since she could hardly go around holding planets, she wore sun and moon earrings.

When the three met up outside the gym, Christopher's eyes said that he recognized the outfit.

As they entered the dance together, the brush of another witch's aura caused Sarah to stretch out a tendril of power and try to locate its source, but the crowd of students was so thick she could not.

A slow song started, and Christopher looked to her. "Want to dance?" he asked as he reached for her hand.

She saw an edge of nervousness in Christopher's expression when she hesitated, and before she could think it through she answered, "Sure."

She tensed when Christopher touched her. Stretching out her senses to locate the other witch had made her hypersensitive to his vampiric aura. He looked so human, so fragile, and yet his presence made her every sense shriek in warning.

She distracted herself by focusing on the other witch. The power she sensed was familiar enough that it made her uneasy. She wasn't supposed to be here, but Dominique wouldn't have come to fetch her, would she? If she was at the dance, or if Adianna was here . . .

Everything about the moment was wrong. At this distance, at this time, Christopher's aura ran over her skin like thousands of spider legs scampering across bare flesh.

She stopped dancing at the same time she saw Adianna in the crowd. How distracted she must have been not to have recognized her sister's presence.

"I can't do this," she whispered, stepping back from Christopher, shaking her head violently. If Adianna saw him, after having given her warning . . .

"What? What did I do?" Christopher asked. The hurt in his eyes was so raw she wanted to comfort him.

But "I'm sorry" was all she could say before she turned away. She who had been taught to fight to the end, win or lose, now ran from one of the very creatures she hunted.

Leaning against the wall outside, completely alone, Sarah felt better. A moment later the doors opened again and Adianna came out, her eyes moving sharply around the area as she checked for any possible threats.

"Sarah, Mother is throwing a fit. She asked me to find you. What are you doing here?" Adianna winced at the obvious answer when the door opened again and Christopher followed them out.

Christopher froze, no doubt sensing danger but not fully understanding it.

"Please, Adia, let me handle this," Sarah asked softly, catching Adianna's wrist before the other hunter could move.

Sarah—Adianna said, reaching out with her mind.

Responding the same way, Sarah interrupted, *I'm going to tell him the truth, and then I'll come home. I care about him, and about his sister. I don't want either of them hurt. Just let me say good-bye my own way. And don't tell Dominique.*

Adianna could read Christopher's aura almost as well as Sarah could, and knew the vampire was not a threat physically. She nodded. If Sarah was going to tell him who she was, and end the friendship, then Adianna would let her do it.

Adianna backed away, keeping her gaze on the vampire until she slipped around the corner to the front of the building.

CHAPTER 10

"WHAT WAS THAT ABOUT?" Christopher asked, bewildered.

"Adianna . . . doesn't like you." It was the most she could think to say. "Come here — away from the door. I need to talk to you, and I don't want someone wandering into our conversation." She led him to the back of the building.

"What did I do?" Christopher asked when she hesitated to explain.

"You"—*are a blood-sucking leech*—"didn't do anything wrong," Sarah answered. She took a breath to brace herself for her next words, because they would hopefully end the closest thing she had ever had to a true friendship. "But I need you to leave me alone." Only seventeen years as Dominique Vida's daughter kept her own pain from her voice. She couldn't continue this double life, and Christopher would be safer knowing nothing. "I want you to stay away from me," she continued, driving the knife home. "Don't talk to me. Don't come near me. Don't even look at me."

"If that's how you feel," he answered, his voice cooler than a moment ago, though she could still hear his hurt in it. She had hidden enough of her own emotions in her life to recognize that he was trying to do the same.

"I'm sorry."

"Don't be—you aren't the first to turn me down, and you probably won't be the last."

"I don't want you getting hurt, Christopher." He shrugged, turning away, as if it didn't matter.

"It's harder to do than one might think," he answered bitterly.

The words gave her a moment of pain. "Christopher, turn around." She couldn't leave him like this, without understanding. She was trying to protect him; she did not want to hurt him.

"I'm leaving. I won't bother you."

"Christopher, look at me!"

He turned around, his face completely neutral except for a hint of anger behind his eyes.

"What?" His voice was cold, controlled — very different from the Christopher that Sarah had come to know. She wondered when in his life he had needed to learn how to show nothing of his thoughts, nothing of his feelings.

"It isn't you," she said quietly. She couldn't stand to let him leave without telling him her reasons. "It isn't who you are . . . and it isn't even what you are. Well, in a way it is, but . . ." She sounded like a bumbling idiot, she knew, but the necessary words did not come easily to her. "It's not just what you are. It's what I am."

Christopher started to ask a question, then paused.

"Christopher, I'm a witch. A Daughter of Macht," she elaborated. Unlike the modern Wiccans, her kind was not human, had never been human.

"I don't care if you're Dominique Vida herself," Christopher declared brazenly.

Christopher's words caused a hysterical giggle to catch in Sarah's throat. Her mother was the most famous — or in vampire circles, infamous — vampire hunter born in hundreds of years.

In answer, she drew the knife from her back; the moon glinted off its silver hilt. Christopher swore under his breath, and she smiled wryly. "Christopher, Dominique is my mother."

Now he looked at her with a small amount of skepticism, which was the last thing she expected. Most vampires were far more wary of her kind. "You? But you're . . ."

She sheathed her knife, trying to show that she meant no threat to him. "I'm what?"

"I've met a lot of hunters in my time, Sarah . . ." He raised a hand, gestured vaguely. "You don't seem like the type."

Stepping forward, she put her right hand flat-palmed against his chest and her left over his throat, pushing him back into the wall.

Shock filled Christopher's features, but then he said, "Your knife is still on your back, and if this was a real fight, we both know I could kill you before you could reach it."

She closed her right fist, drawing Christopher's attention to its position above his heart, and then moved her hand to the wall.

With her mind she reached out and triggered the spring on the knife she wore on her wrist, and the blade snapped out, slicing two inches into the wood paneling of the wall.

"Don't underestimate me, Christopher."

"Are you going to kill me, Sarah?" he asked, but there was no fear in his voice — just an edge of anger. He was getting defensive, trying not to let his hurt show. She recognized the act; anger was much less painful to feel than the sorrow.

"I'm not going to kill you. I don't want my *family* to."

"I can take care of myself." So fearless. Most vampires were afraid of her kind, but Christopher did not seem the least bit worried.

"Meaning what? If my mother or sister attacks you, you'll kill her? There is no good situation here, except for you to leave me alone. I'm not right for you."

"Sarah, I don't care who you are," he repeated. "I've taken a knife from one of your line before. I have a scar, but I'm still alive. If someone attacks me, I leave. That's how I've survived for more than fifty years."

She flinched. How had he taken a Vida knife and lived?

That question was shoved from her mind as she processed the comment about "fifty years." According to the story Nissa had told, he was easily three times that old.

She bit back her questions, and focused on the issue at hand.

"Christopher, maybe you don't care, but I have to."

"You're a teenager—it's your job to act out against your parents. What's the worst they could do to you?" The question was shockingly naïve.

"The worst? Christopher, you don't understand. I am Sarah Tigress Vida, youngest Daughter of Vida. If my mother finds out I have befriended a vampire, she will *disown* me. I'll lose my title, my name, my weapons, and even my magic."

"That could be rough, but you're strong enough to get through it," Christopher said, still not understanding.

"I would be defenseless. I've killed too

many of your kind before. I've made a lot of enemies. If I can't fight back, I'm dead. If my line disowned me, it would be the same as them killing me."

"That's why you want me to leave you alone?"

She paused for only a moment. "They'll kill you, too, if they see you with me again. Maybe you're willing to risk that, but I'm not. I would hate myself for doing it, but I need to defend myself, so if you come near me again, I will have to act."

For an instant, some trick of shadow combined with Sarah's guilt made Christopher look not like a friend who had been betrayed, but like an enemy who had been wronged.

"Fine," he answered, and now his voice was like a steel door, closing on some of the best times Sarah had ever had.

CHAPTER 11

AS SOON AS Christopher was out of sight, Sarah ran from the school grounds, vaulted into the driver's seat of her car, and put the key in the ignition. Her hands were trembling; as soon as she noticed, the movement ceased.

Sarah Tigress Vida was not perfect, but she hadn't lost control since her father had died, and she didn't intend to now.

But she absolutely could not face her family right now. Dominique and Adianna were the last people she wanted to see. Neither did she care to see the other vampire hunters with whom her family would be celebrating the New Year.

At nearly eleven o'clock, she pulled into the brightly lit parking lot of SingleEarth Haven. The mishmash of brilliant auras seeped out of the magically protected building—vampires, shapeshifters, witches, and humans.

She found Caryn near the door. The healer took one look at Sarah and led her to an empty room.

"Why the gloom?" Caryn asked gently, as Sarah collapsed onto the bed.

When Sarah did not answer, Caryn put a hand on her shoulder, friendly despite the fact that they had never been friends. The other witch's aura was like a warm breeze, gentle and soothing as it brushed over Sarah's skin.

"Sarah, what's wrong?"

"Can I just stay here tonight? I can't face my mother right now." Sarah grimaced. "If I don't come home tonight, she's going to want to know where I've been. She'll be upset if I miss the gathering, but it's not against the law for me to be here."

Caryn sat on the bed next to the flustered

hunter. "So long as you're here peacefully, you're welcome to stay. But I would have thought you'd want to spend the New Year with your family."

Sarah closed her eyes, trying to clear from her mind Christopher's expression. "There are some things I need to think through before I see them again. And I don't want to fight with Dominique on a holiday."

Caryn patted her hand. "Stay as long as you like. If you're feeling up to it, you should come downstairs, meet some of the others. Even a hunter needs peace in her life sometimes."

"And how would SingleEarth react to a hunter in their midst?" Sarah asked dryly.

"If you walk in there, some vampires will be nervous, but they'll give you a chance." Sarah laughed, but Caryn went on, saying, "It's the effort that matters. Every vampire, every witch, still has a human soul."

Sarah hesitated, but spending the night alone in this little room, listening to the music from downstairs and staring out the window, was not how anyone would want to spend a holiday.

Caryn led her downstairs, where the

SingleEarth party was bustling with activity. Humans mingled with vampires and witches, laughing and joking together as if they were all the same kind.

Sarah rotated her shoulders, trying to work the tension from between her shoulder blades. No matter how light and happy the revelers were, she kept expecting to feel a knife in her back.

"Loosen up, Sarah," Caryn encouraged her. "Introduce yourself to someone, and ask him to dance. Just have fun. SingleEarth is a safe, neutral place—no one's going to bite."

Despite Caryn's urging, Sarah's feeling of being misplaced refused to fade. She did not join the party, but watched from the edge, until at nearly two o'clock in the morning there was some excitement outside. Someone grabbed Caryn's arm, pulling her toward the doorway.

Caryn paused when she saw whatever it was that stood beyond the door, but she quickly gathered herself and stepped outside, with Sarah hurrying after.

The yard was bright, and Sarah recognized the figure that was leading Caryn toward a dark corner. She trailed behind unobtrusively, not wanting to speak with Christopher if she could help it, but not willing to leave Caryn alone with any non-SingleEarth vampire, even one that she knew. Christopher had blood on his arm, and a small streak of it on his cheek as if he had brushed hair out of his face without realizing his hand was bloody.

Christopher had driven to the party, which was odd in itself, since he, like even the weakest of vampires, could have traveled more easily with his mind. He was driving a sleek white Le Sabre that Sarah had never seen before. She understood instantly, though, when he opened the door to the backseat to reveal an injured human.

Sarah relaxed a bit when she realized Christopher was here to help a human friend, but then her suspicions rose. How had the girl been injured in the first place?

Caryn slipped into the car, ignoring the blood, while Christopher knelt beside the open door.

"Apparently she was at a bash, and she got into a fight," he explained quickly. "One of the vampires there asked me to get her help."

"Why didn't he bring her himself?" Caryn

asked, her voice faint, as most of her concentration went to examining the human.

"Just help her," was all Christopher said in answer.

A second later, Sarah heard Caryn's breath hiss in with surprise.

Curious, Sarah stepped forward to look into the car.

The girl's naturally smooth, dark skin was marred by bruises and shallow wounds, and Sarah could tell that the unconscious victim's jaw was probably broken. She was bleeding in several places, and her breathing was quick and shallow.

Sarah could only see the girl's right arm, but that was enough. Faded scars marked her skin—a rose on her right shoulder and a strand of ivy on her wrist. This girl was one of Nikolas's victims. Had Nikolas beaten her, or had some other vampire caused this more recent injury?

And what was Christopher doing with Nikolas?

"Sarah, Christopher, give me some room," Caryn ordered. Her voice was soft, but the authority was unmistakable. Sarah could feel the gentle pulse of magic emanating from the healer—a warm, peaceful glow, so different from the painful Vida magic.

Sarah could see tension in Christopher's movements as he slipped past her without a word, and moved further away from the light.

"Who is she?"

Christopher paused. "Her name is Marguerite," he answered cautiously. "They asked me to take her, because no one in that group is allowed within a hundred yards of SingleEarth."

"Why you?"

"Probably because they could find me." His voice was growing cooler. "Blood calls to blood—a lot of the people in my line are in that circuit." The words seemed a challenge, as he flaunted his connection to the killers.

She glanced at the car, where Caryn was still working. "What happened to her?"

Christopher shook his head. "I didn't see it. All I know is that another vampire insulted Nikolas, and Marguerite took a swing at him. She nearly got herself killed before someone dragged the two of them apart."

So Nikolas wasn't the one who hurt her, Sarah

thought, almost disappointed. If Nikolas had caused this, Sarah could probably have gotten some information from the girl, but if she had attacked a vampire in defense of Nikolas, then Marguerite was not likely to tell much of anything to a hunter.

"You know Nikolas, then?" she asked aloud.

"Don't, Sarah." Christopher's voice was sure, and made it very clear that he had no intention of telling her anything.

"Were you at the bash?"

"Do you think I'm the one who hit her?" Christopher asked, his voice quiet, but taut with anger.

No, she did not think Christopher would ever hurt a human. But if he was hanging out around Nikolas and other killers, then she would have to start wondering if her impressions were correct. "Did you?"

"I didn't hurt her," he said, turning away. "I wasn't at the bash. I don't follow that circuit." He sounded hurt.

"I had to ask." But that was a lie. She could read his aura, and more than that, she knew Christopher. He wasn't a killer.

Sarah had nothing more to say to him.

Dominique or Adianna would have had a knife to his throat immediately, demanding information on Nikolas and his group. Had he been speaking to any Daughter of Vida but Sarah, Christopher would not have lived through the next five minutes.

The tense silence lasted for several moments, until Caryn called for Christopher to take the girl home. Marguerite needed rest, but she would be fine.

Sarah didn't know what bothered her more—that Christopher had been so frosty, or that she was watching two people who could have given her information on Nikolas drive away from her.

CHAPTER 12

CHRISTOPHER WAS NOT IN CLASS on Monday. The seat next to Sarah in history was painfully empty. No new poems showed up in her locker or in her backpack.

In sculpture class, she avoided Nissa. She knew that if she allowed herself to maintain even a casual in-school relationship with the vampires, she would never be able to keep the necessary distance that Vida law demanded.

By lunch she was surprised to realize she already missed them fiercely. She didn't even go into the cafeteria, but brought her sandwich out to the courtyard and ate on the grass, alone.

In calculus, she began to worry about Christopher. Again he wasn't in class. Vampires did not get sick, and it took a lot to even injure them. While it was possible that Christopher had just decided to avoid school—and her—she hoped that wasn't the case. He had been genuinely enjoying playing human; she didn't want to think that she had chased him away from it.

Of course, if he hadn't planned to be absent, then she didn't like to think about why he wasn't here. While human myth often ascribed to vampires the title "immortal," Sarah well knew they could be killed.

Sarah's resolve not to talk to Nissa might have held, had she not run into the girl in the parking lot after school. She was hurrying to meet up with Caryn to have her cast removed when she nearly collided with Nissa.

Jumping back, she asked, "Is Christopher okay?" The words were out of her mouth before she had a chance to think them through.

Nissa hesitated, apparently surprised. "I

think so. He . . . was upset after the dance, and went to visit his brother. He came home and crashed a little after sunrise this morning."

"His brother?" Sarah parroted, her stomach plummeting. She leaned back against a nearby car, running her hands through her hair. They had made it clear earlier that Christopher's twin had not decided to follow the same peaceful route as his siblings. "Look, Nissa—"

"Excuse me." The voice was dry, and decidedly unhappy. Sarah turned to see Robert, standing sulkily a few feet back. "That's my car you're leaning against."

Nissa grabbed Sarah's arm and pulled her away from the car. Robert went around to the driver's side and popped the trunk.

"I don't know what to make of Robert," Nissa said under her breath, softly so the human would not overhear. "Christopher stumbled across him last night at the bash when he went to help Marguerite."

After that, Sarah stopped paying attention, because quite suddenly she realized where she had seen Robert before she had joined this school. Her barely healed arm was a testament to the night.

"Excuse me, Nissa." No matter what happened, she was a hunter first. Robert had been at the bash where Sarah had run into one of Nikolas's victims, as well as at the bash where Marguerite had been. If he was part of that circuit, then she had a chance to get back to it.

She turned her back on Nissa and hurried to Robert's car, where he was just opening the driver-side door.

"Robert!" She closed the door with one flat palm, and the human jumped, moving his fingers in just enough time to avoid having them slammed in the door.

He tried to ignore her, reaching for the door handle, but he had not accounted for her strength. She wasn't as strong as a vampire, but she could easily outmuscle a pure-blood human.

"What do you want?" he finally asked.

Sarah glanced back to where Nissa had been, but the girl had disappeared. With no one to overhear, she answered Robert's question honestly. "I want to know what you were doing at a bash on Halloween night."

"I was invited," Robert snapped.

"By who?"

"Can't you just read my mind or something?" He shouldered her aside, and the mixture of his words and the movement forced her off balance enough that she let him.

He thought she was a vampire. Oh, that was rich. Nearly laughing, she caught the door before he had a chance to get in the car.

"Robert, you have no idea what you're talking about—"

"Leave me *alone*."

"I'm not a vampire." Her mind was working quickly. He had seen her at the bash, and had made the obvious assumption. What she couldn't figure out was why, if he thought she was a vampire, he had hated her almost on sight. Though there were always plenty of humans who were invited to a bash purely as entrees, most repeat guests attended because they *liked* being fed on. Robert obviously wasn't part of the first group, but his aversion to her proved that he wasn't part of the second, either.

The only other humans who attended bashes were blood bonded, or thought themselves hunters. Sarah would have sensed a blood bond.

"Then what are you?" Robert pressed. "You sure as hell aren't human."

"I'm a witch."

Robert snorted. "And pigs fly."

He had just begun to slide into the seat when she added, "And I'm a vampire hunter."

Finally the human paused, and again she sensed him sizing her up.

Technically, Sarah should have asked Dominique's permission before telling any human she was a witch. Depending on how Robert handled her revelation, Sarah would either have to wipe his mind to make him forget she had said anything—something that was difficult, but possible—or she might be able to enlist his help.

Robert glanced around the parking lot, where other students were gathering in the postschool flurry of activity. "Get in the car," he finally said. "Tell me what you know."

He pulled out of the parking lot before Sarah could think how to begin. Her silence seemed to make him uneasy, so he spoke instead. "Look. Just because I'm listening to you doesn't necessarily mean I believe you.

But maybe if you tell me what you were doing at the bash . . ."

"You must have left early if you don't know
the answer to that one," Sarah said, thinking
of the disaster that night had turned into.

"About ten," Robert answered, with a
nod. "I couldn't find the person I was looking for, so it made sense to ditch."

"Who were you looking for?"

Robert had been driving aimlessly, apparently, but now he stopped at the side of the
road. Voice cool and level despite the suspicion, he asked, "Why do you care?"

Sarah could see he wasn't going to give
away information for free, and unlike the
vampires, she did not have the ability to
reach into his mind and find what she
needed to know. She had to tell him something. "I want someone dead, and you might
be able to help me," she explained.

Robert hesitated for only a fraction of a
heartbeat. "You're after Nikolas." When
Sarah nodded, he looked at her with absolute
skepticism, sizing up her slender figure. "You
really think you could get that . . . creature?"

"I'm going to try," she snapped before she
could catch herself. His implication had

struck a chord, but Robert didn't know what he was talking about; getting mad at him wouldn't help things. She forced herself to control her tone the next time she spoke. "I'm not planning to arm wrestle him, Robert, and I'm not as helpless as you think. I'm not human; I'm stronger than your kind, and I have more power. And I've been trained to kill vampires my entire life. I know what I'm doing."

"Well, good luck," Robert answered sarcastically. "I've killed my share of vampires, but I've still been after this bastard for months."

She had to restrain herself from snickering at his bravado as she noticed Robert hadn't elaborated on the exact number of leeches he had put a knife through. She wasn't surprised. He was only human, after all, and though she hadn't seen him fight, his ignorance of her kind told Sarah that he was probably relatively new at wielding a knife. He was lucky he had not run into Nikolas yet, or his little extracurricular activity would have gotten him killed already.

"How long have you been hunting?" she asked.

"Since Nikolas." His response was short, but clear.

"What did he do to you?"

Robert took a deep breath, his gaze somewhere past Sarah's left shoulder. "Not to me . . . my sister." He spoke slowly, considering his words carefully before they emerged. "Her name was Christine."

"Was?" Sarah would be far from surprised to learn the leech had slaughtered the poor girl.

"We call her Kristin, now. She doesn't respond to her real name." He paused. The silence was so long that Sarah began to wonder if he was finished, but finally he continued, "One of her friends, Heather, brought her to a party . . . I didn't know then, but it was one of Nikolas's bashes. She didn't come home that night, or the next morning. My mother called the police, and they must have checked the hospitals." Again he took a deep breath as if to brace himself, and she could see the vision forming in his eyes. "She had lost a lot of blood. He had carved his name into her arms, then left her nearly dead on some stranger's front lawn."

As he spoke, emotions surged across

Robert's aura—fury, frustration, hatred. He forced his lungs to take in a deep breath of air to calm himself, but it did no good. "At first she was just scared and skittish when she got home. She wouldn't let us call her Christine anymore, and she stayed in her room all the time. If you asked her, she would talk about Nikolas, about how . . . handsome and gentle he was." The last words were spat like a curse. "She always described him as black and white, and after a while she made herself that way too. She shudders away from anything colorful, and she screams when she sees anything red."

Sarah didn't like doing it, but she probed his memory wound for useful information. Robert would have to deal with the pain if he wanted to help his sister. "Is that all you know?"

"Only that it gets worse every day. No doctor has been able to help her." He shook his head. "I went to the house where the bash had been a few days after Kristin got home, but it was collapsing in flame. There was this old man watching the fire—he lived next door, and invited me in for iced tea. Said the vampires had been living beside him for years. Usually, he said, he didn't mind unless they put the music on really loud. But when they left Kristin on his lawn, he got fed up and torched the place ..." Bitterly, Robert added, "He had known all along what they were, and what was going on over there. But he hadn't gotten angry until they trampled his garden when they left Kristin. *That's* when he acted."

Sarah found herself pulling back from the human, who was trembling with rage strong enough to make her head spin. Yet she forced herself to say, "Robert, I need to talk to Kristin."

He gave her a you-have-got-to-be-kidding-me look. "She doesn't talk to any-one, not even me."

Sarah wanted to argue further, but held back. A visit now would be wasted. She needed time to think of a way to approach Kristin so the girl would talk to her.

Robert gave her a ride home, and as they arrived Sarah took a pad of paper from her backpack. Scribbling down her phone num-ber, she ripped out the sheet and handed it to Robert. "Give me a call sometime soon." Hesitantly, she added, "You really should talk to my mother, too. She can train you to fight." Sarah did not know if the human would admit he needed help, but Robert wasn't going to live long if he wasn't trained.

As she slid out of the car, Robert grabbed her arm. "Wait just a sec." He paused, then seemed to make up his mind. "If you really think you have a chance at him, I have something for you."

He tore off the bottom of the paper where she had written her number, and jotted down an address. "I was at a bash here on Halloween. I left when a fight broke out, but I was there long enough to know it's his house. It's about two hours away."

Sarah smiled, glad for the first bit of truly helpful information Robert had been able to supply. Soon she would be facing one of the longest-hunted vampires in the Vida records. Not even Dominique and Adianna would be able to belittle *that* fight.

"Thanks."

"Tell me how it goes?"

With a nod, she closed the car door. She was glad her cast was coming off tonight.

CHAPTER 13

SARAH SKIPPED SCHOOL the next day. Posing as her mother, she called early and excused herself.

No well-trained hunter was mad enough to stalk a vampire on his own turf at night. While real vampires were not confined to coma-like, coffin-enclosed sleeps whenever the sun was up, they were naturally nocturnal. Christopher and Nissa were prime examples that vampires could function fine in the daylight world, but the stronger a vampire grew, the more irritating sunlight became, and the less natural a diurnal schedule was.

So she was fairly sure that at ten o'clock in

the morning, Nikolas would be asleep. At least he would be alone, and not hosting a bash. She wasn't suicidal enough to approach him in a group of his kind, but she believed she could handle one vampire on her own—even the legendary Nikolas.

When she reached the address Robert had given her, she drove past it once, checking for lights and sounds. It was hard to tell over the vampiric aura that saturated the area, but she thought she sensed humans inside.

The next time around the block, she parked down the street. She stopped the Jaguar at the boundary of two property lines, so if either of the houses' owners saw her, they would each assume she was a guest of the other.

Breaking into a house at ten o'clock in the morning was not generally a good idea, but somehow she doubted she would be welcome if she simply knocked on the door. Swathing herself in magic, she approached through the side yard. If a human glanced in her direction, he would see her movement as the rustle of leaves in a breeze. She wasn't invisible, but humans saw a great deal that they didn't consciously notice. She hoped her magic would keep her safe from detection of the blood bonded humans inside as well, since if any of them saw her, the vampire would shortly follow.

The house was upper middle class, nondescript but for a string of clematis that bloomed a brilliant violet around the mailbox and wraparound porch. Trees grew heavily in this neighborhood, providing plenty of shade in which simple plants grew. Someone had devoted time to gardening.

The image of a long-hunted vampire practicing horticulture was amusing enough to bring a smile to her face, although she doubted he was the gardener.

From the yard, she sized up the house. It was three stories, four if it had a basement. The top floor had a large bay window on the northern side, but white curtains blocked Sarah's view.

After a quick check to make sure all her knives were in place, Sarah swung onto the porch, her sneakers barely making a sound. A quick burst of laughter alerted her just before two girls came around the corner of the house. Focusing her power, Sarah threw a burst of it at the two, the magical equivalent of a hammer to the head. Both girls collapsed, instantly unconscious. They would wake awhile later, groggy but unharmed.

Taking a deep breath to regain her focus, Sarah stepped past the girls and slipped through the open door they had just exited.

Instantly she felt color-blind. *Black and white,* Robert had said. She was in the right place.

The carpet of the living room was plush black. The walls were white but for abstract designs that had been painted onto them in black. The furniture was a combination of black and white.

Her head nearly spinning at the abrupt change of scenery, Sarah barely avoided knocking a vase of white roses off a black table. Their green leaves were the only bit of color in the room.

She passed through the first floor quickly, easily satisfied that it was empty. On the second floor she passed one door behind which she sensed another human. This one was probably sleeping, but Sarah didn't risk checking. The rest of the house was empty but for the vampire she sensed on the top floor, probably in the room with the bay window.

Climbing another flight of stairs, she sensed him very close by. If he was sleeping, she still had a chance to surprise him. More likely he had already sensed her the same way she could sense him, and was expecting to fight.

She opened the door that she knew must lead to Nikolas's room, but what she found there threw her entirely off balance.

The walls were pure art, covered with pictures drawn in careful black paint, like a sketch enlarged to become a mural.

And she *recognized* the figures. Kaleo and Kendra, and other high-society vampiric killers, each in aloof portraits, graced the walls. Worse, she recognized her friends— Christopher and Nissa.

Still dazed, she spun when she sensed someone behind her.

Christopher?

He was dressed entirely in black—black boots, black jeans, and a black T-shirt. His hair was much longer than it had been when she saw him last, and the ebony waves were tied back.

He looked exactly the same except for the hair, but something was very *wrong*.

His expression was dark and angry, as opposed to the open, smiling one she had grown so fond of. But the wrongness didn't reach her brain until he pushed her back into the wall, forcing the breath from her lungs. The vampire's aura washed over her like ice water — too strong, too dark. Christopher did not feed on humans, but this vampire did, and probably had for more than a hundred years.

So this is the brother, she found herself thinking. She remembered how Nissa and Christopher had clammed up when she had tried to inquire about Christopher's twin. *Would have been nice to know before stumbling in here.*

Too late — she had hesitated for that vital instant and now Nikolas had the advantage. He grabbed both her wrists with one of his hands and held them against the wall, careful to avoid the spring-loaded knife she was wearing on her left arm. He stood to her side, carefully out of kicking range.

Sarah was concentrating, preparing to strike him with her mind, when his free hand came from nowhere and hit her.

"Don't try it, Sarah." His voice was similar

to Christopher's—a slight southern accent, so like the one she had come to trust.

She pulled her mind away from Nikolas's family—he was a threat, and that was all that mattered.

Yet he wasn't doing anything threatening at the moment. Instead, he was regarding her with curiosity. "Sarah Vida, I presume?" he inquired, voice civil.

"Making sure introductions are out of the way before we fight?" she asked flippantly.

"I'll admit I'm flattered to have such a prestigious hunter track me down," he answered calmly, "but I haven't the faintest idea how to deal with you."

That threw her off guard. So far as she knew, there was only one way vampires "dealt with" hunters who entered their lairs.

"Want to hear my suggestions?" she asked, voice light, the words a cover as she started to raise power again.

He raised one eyebrow. "I don't think we're—" He broke off and hit her again, the blow making her head spin. "I said not to try it."

So he could feel her building power; that much was obvious. She would simply have to wait for a chance when he was distracted, which meant she might need to wait for him to bite her.

"If you're going to kill me, go ahead. If you're waiting for me to scream or beg, your expectations are way off."

"Your control is really that good?" She heard in his voice that he had taken her words as a challenge.

It was a challenge she knew she could win. He could break her neck easily if he wanted to, but if he wanted to hear her scream, he would have to hurt her. Badly. That would take time, and time would give her a chance to escape. "Yes, it is."

Nikolas pulled a knife from his pocket: an ivory-handled jackknife with a rose inlay made of black stone. Opening it, he pressed it against her left wrist, just hard enough for her to feel the sharpness of the blade against her skin.

"If that's supposed to be a threat, it won't work," she informed him as he glanced to her face as if to gauge her expression. "A cut there would bleed out quickly. If you mean to feed on me, you won't waste so much blood."

"And if I just mean to kill you?" he inquired.

"You would have done so already," she answered, her voice calm despite her uncertainty.

"You sure you won't beg?" he asked, offering her one last chance to avoid pain.

"Quite sure."

Still holding her wrists with his right hand, he held the knife in his left hand, and pressed the blade into her shoulder—one sharp cut, about an inch in length.

Her muscle twitched as the knife cut through it, but Sarah refused to let pain show on her face. She used her training in order to not react, since he was looking for a response. She could take a lot of damage and heal from it. Sooner or later, he would slip up, and then he would be dead.

He pulled the knife upward, this cut at a slight angle to the last one, and then down again, as if making a Z.

Or an N.

The next cut was just beside the last line of the first letter, a half-inch line, and the next was a line parallel to the second letter. She knew what he was writing, and sighed, realizing this could be a long night. Two more short lines followed the most recent, making a K, and then a rough, squared-off circle.

Nikolas.

If it scarred, she was going to be really annoyed.

"Is your control really this good, or are you a secret masochist?" Nikolas asked as he cut the tail of the S, a jagged underline.

"Is this a ritual thing, or are you just a sadist?" she returned, impatient. Though he was enjoying his busywork, he wasn't focused enough for Sarah to act.

"Both," he answered, laughing, as he turned to the other arm. "You can ask me to stop any time now." She understood what he really meant—*You can break down and beg.* "Or must I continue?"

"Hurry up, would you?" She yawned. "I have to get to the drugstore before it closes. We're out of Band-Aids at my house."

Nikolas laughed. "Don't worry about that—you won't need them."

The rose petals were more difficult, and Nikolas did not say anything as he worked on them. When he moved to the ivy she took a deep breath, preparing herself. The ivy's stem twined around the wrist; in order to cut the full design, Nikolas would need to shift his grip.

Her arms had gone numb from the abuse and from being held above her head so long, which was actually a good thing. The pain was dulling.

"I hope that blade is clean. I would hate for this to get infected." She spoke to break the silence and keep hold of her bravado.

As she had predicted, Nikolas loosened his grip for a split second, and Sarah seized her moment, wrenching her arms down and drawing her knife at the same time. Nikolas only barely managed to avoid the silver blade as she swung it in his direction.

"You're not as quick as some of your kin, Sarah," he informed her, from just outside striking distance.

She laughed slightly. "Quick enough."

"Quicker than Elisabeth?" he inquired, and her eyes narrowed as she remembered the long hours of history. Nikolas was one of very few vampires who had killed a Vida and survived to speak of it.

"How much of a fight did she put up?"

Sarah snapped. "Did she at least get a knife in you before she died?"

"Not in me." The words were almost a growl. "Get out of my house, Sarah. I will see you shortly."

He disappeared before she could react.

As she relaxed, the knife fell from her numb fingertips. She picked it up with her left hand, which wasn't much better.

She leaned back against the wall and stretched out her awareness. While she had been occupied with Nikolas, the humans in the house had fled—even the ones she had knocked out were gone.

Her stomach churned with the unpleasant nausea that comes with blood loss. After bandaging her arms as well as she could with the scant supplies she kept in the car, she picked up her cell phone and dialed Adianna.

CHAPTER 14

ADIANNA TOOK SARAH to Caryn Smoke's house, to be patched up for the second time in less than a month. Sarah had managed to fend off her sister's questions only with stoic silence so far.

"We're going to have to wash the blood off before I can see the cuts," Caryn explained as she unwrapped the crude bandages Sarah had made with the rough first-aid supplies she kept in her car.

She had cleaned most of the blood from the ivy before she could see enough to tell what the full design was.

"Oh, Goddess . . ." The healer looked up,

her pale blue eyes wide with shock and full of question.

"What?" Adianna stepped forward to see what the healer had seen.

"Give me some room," Caryn ordered, her voice steady.

Adianna nodded, and leaned back against the opposite wall.

Caryn turned to the rose. When she got to the other shoulder she cleaned around the wound, revealing more of the damage.

Nikolas. Caryn whispered the name, and Sarah saw Adianna's gaze whip toward them as she heard it.

The hunter was on her feet instantly. "*That's* who you were after today?" Sarah nodded once, and saw Adianna's eyes racing over the careful designs. Finally she asked Caryn the question Sarah had been avoiding. "Will those scar?"

Caryn's face was grim as she said, "I'm afraid so. I can heal the deeper damage so there won't be any permanent injury to the muscles, but the wounds are bad enough that I can't do much more."

"My little sister went after Nikolas," Adianna stated with some surprise in her voice.

"He got away, didn't he?" Again Sarah had to nod.

"He's had hunters on his tail for more than a hundred years, Adia—he's clever, and he could feel when I tried to build power to fight him. I didn't have a chance."

Yes, you did, another part of her mind argued as she remembered her moment of hesitation when she had first seen him. *But he looked like Christopher, so you didn't take it.*

Adianna just shook her head, making her feelings clear: If Sarah had not had a chance to fight, it meant she had screwed up somewhere. Again.

CHAPTER 15

CARYN BANDAGED SARAH'S ARMS for school the next day. Sarah didn't want to explain the marks. Her story, when anyone asked, was that she had been in a minor car accident.

She was glad that Christopher was not in school again. She had no desire to confront her friend about her enemy. So at her locker that afternoon, she was surprised to see the newest gift. A single white rose and a small white florist's card.

129 Ash Road, November 4

She read the words twice, not believing them.

She, youngest Daughter of Vida, had been invited to a bash . . . *intentionally.*

Looking up, she caught sight of Nissa, who was talking with some of her human friends. Closing her locker, Sarah stalked over to Nissa and grabbed the vampire's arm.

"What is this?" she demanded, flashing the card. Nissa's friends all backed up, not sure what to do.

"It's a—"

"I know *what* it is. I want to know why it was in my locker."

"I have no idea," Nissa answered, her brows drawing together in a puzzled frown. "Christopher told me what you said, and I would never . . . can I see it?"

Sarah handed over the card and Nissa went paler, if possible, than her already un-naturally pale color.

"You can't go. Tell me you won't go."

"Why not?"

Nissa looked at the card again. "Where did you get this?"

"It was in my locker. If it's not from you or Christopher, then who would have put it there? And why does it scare you so much?"

Nissa looked back at her human friends, then dragged Sarah away, lowering her voice so the humans would not hear them. "I've been to a bash in that circuit before, but would never go back. Sarah, they'll kill you. If they know who you are—"

"Who are *they*?" Sarah pressed.

"It's . . . it's one of the harshest of the party circuits," Nissa explained. "Tizoc Theron goes to these," she added, naming one of the best-known vampiric assassins in the world. "Kaleo, Jessica Shade, Chalkha, Kamerine, Jega . . . even Kendra herself might be there." Sarah took in the names, trying to match them with the faces she had seen at the last bash she had attended. Nissa continued, "Even *I'm* afraid to go to one of their bashes, and I haven't been human in a long time. These vampires are *not nice,* Sarah. I've known them to brazenly invite vampire hunters just for the fun of it. If they invited you, then they know who you are, and they plan to kill you."

"Is Nikolas part of this group?"

"What?" Nissa asked, very softly.

"Will Nikolas be there?" Sarah demanded again.

"He—" Nissa's eyes flickered to the bandages on Sarah's arms. "My god, Sarah . . . do I want to know what's under there?"

"I think you already do."

"You're going to go, aren't you? To murder my brother." Nissa leaned back heavily, hitting the lockers with a metallic clang. "That group will kill you, Sarah."

"They didn't manage to last time." This was not a conversation she wanted to have. No matter how peaceful, Nissa would surely not appreciate hearing Sarah's plans for her brother. "Don't worry, I'll bring friends."

"*No.*"

"I'm not going to let him get away with this."

"Sarah, I . . . don't bring anyone else in. You'll—" Nissa took a breath to brace herself. "If Nikolas marked you then he's watching you. Anyone you would bring with you, he already knows about—they would be fair game. If you insist on going, go alone."

"Even I'm not fool enough to go into the crowd you're describing alone."

"They won't hurt you," Nissa said quietly.

Sarah laughed.

"Most of the people in that circuit are either afraid of Nikolas, or loyal to him," Nissa argued. "If he marked you it means he's claimed you. No one else will touch you so long as Nikolas is alive."

"Fine — I'll kill him and then leave quickly. How's that?"

"Nikolas alone is dangerous no matter how much training you've had." Nissa continued as her voice took on a pleading tone. "Even the humans there will turn on you as soon as you try to fight him."

"Nissa, I know he's your brother, but do you have any idea how many people he has killed?" Sarah demanded. "If I let him go because I'm scared of him, he's going to keep killing."

"You think I don't know?" Nissa responded, her voice strained. "I'm the one who gave him the vampire blood, Sarah. Every kill he makes *I* feel the guilt for."

CHAPTER 16

"WHAT?" Of course she had known, but hearing Nissa state it so bluntly was a shock.

"I changed him to save his life. He was in jail, waiting to be hanged for murder." In response to Sarah's horrified expression, Nissa continued, "He was my *brother*, Sarah."

Nissa's words started to come quickly, as if she had waited so long to tell the story to *someone*, and now she simply needed to get it out.

"Nicholas and Christopher were twins, as you know . . . Christopher was actually born first, but Nicholas always acted older. After my father was killed, Nicholas . . . he became more protective. Christopher had barely understood what happened, but Nicholas . . ." She trailed off. The reality of Nikolas did not need to be detailed.

"When they were eighteen their employer's daughter returned from school in Europe. She was rich, and beautiful, and both my brothers adored her, though Nicholas would never have challenged Christopher for anything.

"She, of course, wasn't interested. We were too poor and too uncultured for her high-society airs. The only reason she even acknowledged my brothers' existences was because it amused her to tease them. She was always trying to pit the twins against one another."

Nissa's gaze was lost on the past, but Sarah caught a glimpse of anger as she described the girl. "Her name was Christine."

Nissa paused a moment and then went on, "It was at a May Day picnic that things changed. Kaleo was well respected in the town and he had found an invitation for us. Nicholas and Christopher looked so handsome, all dressed up. They had taken extra care to look nice for Christine.

"Christopher asked her to dance." Nissa's voice gave away the next part of the story even before she said the words. She took a heavy breath and then continued, "Christine turned him down. Worse, she laughed at him. The things she said to my brother . . . I would have killed her myself, if I had had a chance.

"Nicholas lost it—he was so protective, and he attacked Christine, furious that she had hurt Christopher. He killed her, in plain sight of the entire town, and was sentenced to be hanged."

"He was my brother." Nissa's eyes begged for understanding. "I had already lost my father, and I could not stand to lose Nicholas, too. Not when I could save him.

"I changed Nicholas, but after that . . . The only thing I've ever been grateful to Kaleo for is that the first time he took me hunting, he didn't let me kill. The police were looking for Nikolas, and while I was trying to deal with them, Nikolas woke. It was the middle of the day, far earlier than he should have woken. He ran, and would have died if one of my kind had not taken him in." Nissa shook her head. "Kendra took him hunting, and she taught him to kill.

"He changed Christopher the next night. They both disappeared from my life for months. Kaleo had everyone he knew looking for them, but no one could find them.

"During that time, they made the decision to give up everything that reminded them of their human lives, and that included me. They even changed how they signed their names." She took a breath, her eyes pained. "They never contacted me. I didn't even know they were still alive until I learned a year later that they had killed a witch, Elisabeth Vida. After that . . . well, they seemed to be everywhere at once."

Nissa met Sarah's gaze, her voice hard. "If you kill once, the bloodlust returns twice as strong. It hurts, and after you've been living off death for more than a hundred years . . . it hurts a lot. You have no idea how hard it was for Christopher to give it up, no idea how tempting every human being in this entire school is.

"I have given everything for my brothers, and they have both saved my life more than once when I wasn't strong enough to defend myself from others of my kind. I would probably never forgive myself for harming a friend—and I do consider you a friend, Sarah—but if you hurt my brother, I *will* kill you, or die trying."

Sarah flinched at the passion in Nissa's voice. "I can't let Nikolas live."

"Sarah, please—" Nissa broke off, as if knowing there was nothing she could say. The vampire disappeared, but Sarah would not allow her determination to waver.

She threw out the rose Nikolas had sent with the invitation. Nissa had taken the card, but Sarah remembered the necessary information. The bash would be tonight, at 129 Ash Road. It wasn't the same house she had found before, but considering his age and notoriety, Sarah was not surprised that Nikolas had more than one.

She wouldn't miss this for the world.

If Nissa was telling the truth, then Sarah would only be in danger from Nikolas . . . until she took him down. There was no need to endanger other hunters. If Nikolas knew who her allies were, he would alert the group immediately, and the other hunters would not have even the scant protection that Nikolas's marks gave to Sarah. *How ironic,* Sarah thought grimly. Nikolas's marks would enable her to kill him.

CHAPTER 17

SARAH FELT A LITTLE GUILT as she lied to Adianna, telling her that she was going to hunt in the relatively safe city.

She wore black jeans and a white tank top, and her jacket hid the bandages, as well as the knife on her left wrist. Her primary knife was on her back, and she had two slim silver daggers in her boots.

Nikolas was playing with her, which meant he would give her a chance to fight. As soon as she had that chance, she would use it. This time there would be no hesitation.

The house appeared dark as Sarah approached it. All the shades were down, but she could hear a haunting melody from inside, a mixture of pain and loneliness. The door opened just as she reached for the knob, and she was again confronted with the peculiar — and powerful — world of Nikolas.

Black and white.

The walls were black with a white design running across them, spiraling and plunging, the lines all slightly wrong, drawing the eye to seemingly impossible shapes. The other house she had seen had been crisp in its lack of color; the abstraction in this one made Sarah's vision spin, so she turned to the vampire who had opened the door for her.

Kaleo's red shirt in the black-and-white interior of Nikolas's house was a startling blot of color. Sarah tensed as she remembered her last encounter with him.

"Sarah Vida, nice to see you again," he said, his voice lilting with sarcasm as she met his black gaze without fear. "Nikolas told us to expect you. You can relax, take your jacket off, and make yourself at home. It's only eleven."

"I don't make myself at home in a place like

this," she answered, and he just laughed and reached over to close the door behind her.

"Sarah, so good to see you."

She looked toward the voice, but her eyes took a moment to differentiate the figure there from the background.

Nikolas was wearing white slacks and a black silk shirt, and his hair was tied back with a black ribbon. He had not yet fed tonight, and the skin that she could see was almost white, pearl-like. Black and white, colorless, he matched the room perfectly. *Is that what his mind is like?* she wondered. *All sharp contrasts without color or emotion?*

"Welcome to my home, Sarah. Please, come away from the door. May I take your jacket?"

This time it was her turn to laugh. "You can drop the act, Nikolas."

"There is no act, Sarah. Acting, like lying, is an art I have never perfected. Come into my parlor."

"Said the spider to the fly," Sarah finished for him, and he smiled, taking her jacket.

"I never kill until the hour, Sarah."

"Am I really supposed to believe that?" she asked skeptically.

"I never lie."

He hung her jacket in the closet and turned his back to her, leading her deeper into the house. She wanted so much to put a knife into his back immediately, but his next words discouraged her.

"What about you, Sarah? I do not kill until midnight. As it is, I'm not sure that I plan to kill you at all. Do you have any rules for yourself, or should we forget all manners and throw ourselves on the mercy of chaos?"

"You want me to wait until midnight to kill you?" she asked incredulously, and Nikolas turned back to face her.

"If that's what you plan to do tonight, then yes, I would like for you to wait until midnight to *try*. You are a guest here this time—you must abide by our rules."

"Hardly." She leaned back against the wall, crossing her arms. Her right hand rested over the handle of the knife strapped to her left wrist, and she was comforted by the cool feel of silver beneath her fingertips.

"Honor, Sarah," Nikolas sighed. "Does the Vida line no longer teach its children honor? I invited you, and you accepted the invitation. It would be rather unsporting to spoil the game because you are impatient."

"I am never impatient."

"Just like you never shout out," he answered. "And never cry, even when you make enemies of your friends. Yes, Nissa told me about your conversation," he said before she could ask. "So, will you follow our rules?"

"I can wait until midnight."

"Do I have your word on that?" he asked, his gaze intense.

She did not answer immediately. When a Vida gave her word, she kept it, so Sarah was careful how she phrased her answer. "Unless you threaten me, I will wait until midnight to kill you. You have my word on that."

Nikolas smiled, and for an instant the expression reminded her of Christopher. "Very well, then. Enjoy the bash—you'll probably never make it to another one."

CHAPTER 18

By ELEVEN-THIRTY, Sarah had been introduced to others, some humans, some vampires. She wondered just how much needed to be done before these killers would drop their social detachment and retaliate, and whether Nikolas even cared that his father's murderer was among the guests.

"Not until midnight." Kaleo's voice slipped through the noise of the room, a hint of laughter in his tone, and Sarah repressed a shiver. She glanced over to see a young woman gazing up at Kaleo with the intensity of love — or terror.

"Midnight is only half an hour away," she argued.

"Is there some hurry, dear?" Kaleo bent his head to kiss his victim's throat; she sighed, leaned her head back, and when he stood again she leaned against a wall, clearly disappointed.

Sarah jumped when she felt hands on her shoulders. "I thought you never reacted," Nikolas said, laughing.

"I'm standing in a slaughterhouse where the cattle are begging to become hamburgers. I have a right to be jumpy."

"Ah." Nikolas followed Sarah's gaze. "Heather is Kaleo's favorite. She has been frequenting these bashes for longer than I have been alive."

"God," Sarah whispered, sickened. A blood bonded human did not age. This girl could remain alive, Kaleo's personal prey, for thousands of years unless he tired of her and killed her. *Or,* Sarah thought, forming an instant hatred of the vampire, *until I kill him.*

"Welcome to my world, Sarah," Nikolas answered. "Why are you wearing these?" He reached to the bandages on her right arm as she pulled away. "Are you ashamed of what they hide?"

"Ashamed?" she echoed, incredulous. "Should I be *proud* to show the world that you've sliced your name into my skin?"

Nikolas laughed. "Look around you."

The comment was well placed. Sarah had already seen several humans with Nikolas's marks on them. When he entered the room, they greeted him with adoration. While they were discreet in human society, in Nikolas's own lair they wore tank shirts or sleeveless dresses, going out of their way to show off the marks.

"I'd rather burn them off, personally," she growled.

"If you really want to, you can always do that later, though I've heard it's painful," Nikolas commented, apparently serious. "Of course, I don't suppose you would mind a little more pain, would you?"

Before she could react he grabbed her wrist, pulling her toward him sharply enough that she stumbled and needed to catch herself on the arm of a nearby couch.

"I thought you played by the rules," she

hissed, snatching her other wrist away when he reached for it.

"I do. I'm simply removing these," Nikolas answered, carefully unwinding the bandage on the wrist he had a hold on.

"Let me go."

He let go of her arms, but continued to undo the bandages until each of his marks was revealed.

The sudden movement had opened one of the cuts on her shoulder, and he bent his head down to the wound. She felt the soft sensation of his lips on her skin and tried to pull away, but Nikolas grabbed her right arm and held her still.

Pressing her left hand to his chest, with the tip of the spring-loaded knife only inches from his heart, she said, "I consider this a threat. Let me go, or I will kill you where you stand."

"You're right," Nikolas said, lifting his head and releasing her. The taste of her blood, stronger and sweeter than any human's, had caused his expression to darken with bloodlust. "It isn't midnight yet, is it?"

CHAPTER 19

"*DAMN*, SARAH."

She spun toward the familiar voice, and nearly swore when she recognized her sister. Kaleo, lounging against one of the walls, watched the confrontation with malicious pleasure—he must have let Adianna in.

"You really have gotten yourself into trouble this time, haven't you, little sister?" Adianna asked, sizing up the situation.

"What are you doing here?" Sarah demanded, frustrated by her sister's appearance. Adianna was going to get herself killed.

"Touchy today, aren't we?" Adianna responded.

"How did you know where I was?"

"I wanted to know what was up with you. I asked this"—she gestured to Nikolas—"thing's brother, Christopher, and he told me you were here."

Sarah cringed inwardly. Adianna didn't *talk* to vampires—if they had information she needed, she would force it from them. Sarah hoped Christopher was still alive.

Evidently, Nikolas had the same thought, because Sarah saw instant hatred on his face. He stepped forward a pace and Adianna drew her knife.

"Come any nearer, and you won't be pleased with the results," Adianna warned.

"Tell you what," Nikolas said slowly, glancing from Adianna to Sarah and then back. The other vampires had disappeared, leaving Nikolas alone with the two hunters and a scattered handful of groggy humans; Sarah could tell he was stalling for time. "Only Sarah is in my plan for tonight. I'll let you leave safely, if you will do so now."

Adianna did not wait for him to continue but attacked instantly. No hesitation, no thought, just pure Vida skill.

Nikolas dodged, but Adianna turned

quickly, cutting into his side. Sarah had just drawn her knife to join the fray when something struck her from behind, sending her stumbling. More astonished than frightened, she twisted and detached the human who had attacked her, knocking the girl out with a small burst of power.

A quick scan revealed two more humans on their feet and ready to fight if necessary, but Nikolas did not need the help. Sarah heard something in Adianna's arm snap as the vampire slammed her back into the wall.

"Nikolas, let her go!" Sarah shouted.

"Why?" he asked, his hand over Adianna's windpipe, ready to crush it.

"Adianna isn't involved in this—she only came because she heard I was here. Let her go."

"Christopher wouldn't have told her where I was unless she hurt him," Nikolas growled.

Sarah advanced, careful to keep the humans from her back, and Nikolas's grip on Adianna's throat tightened. "The hour has fallen, Sarah—I could kill her before you could get near enough to hurt me, and you know it."

"Then how about I leave now, while you are busy with her?" Sarah bluffed. "It would ruin your plans for tonight, wouldn't it?"

Nikolas hesitated. "I suppose it would dent them a bit."

"Let her go, Nikolas." Adianna was turning blue from Nikolas's grip, and it took all of Sarah's will not to attack.

"You are in no place to make demands, Sarah, but I'll make a deal with you anyway. Marguerite?"

One of the humans answered. "Yes?"

Sarah spared a glance and recognized the girl from SingleEarth. Nikolas's marks on her dark skin looked like pearl inlays.

It was not these designs, though, that sent dread down Sarah's spine. There were two more on her left arm, which must have been tucked under the girl when she had been brought to SingleEarth: one was a teardrop, and the other was a second signature.

Kristopher.

"Sarah," Nikolas said, "Give your knives—all of them—to Marguerite so she can bring them upstairs, and I will let your sister go safely."

She believed him. However warped,

somewhere within Nikolas's twisted mind was a sense of honor.

Of course, if she relinquished all her weapons, Nikolas would probably kill *her*. And it was *completely* against Vida rules to surrender arms to any leech.

"Fine," she answered, drawing the first knife from her back.

Nikolas loosened his grip on Adianna's throat enough that she could breathe, and Adianna immediately said through her teeth, "Sarah, what are you *doing*?"

She did not answer.

Adianna had never broken the rules. She hadn't befriended the vampires or made deals with them. She hadn't revealed her powers to a human boy. Stronger and colder, Adianna was the one more likely to survive after this night, and so Sarah had to do what she could to help her. The Vida line had to go on, and Adianna was a better Vida than Sarah could ever be.

It seemed to take a long time before Sarah had finished stripping herself of weapons, but it was all too soon that Nikolas asked Marguerite to bring them upstairs, and Sarah was left standing before the vampire unarmed. Nikolas pulled Adianna away from the wall and disappeared with her.

He reappeared alone in an instant. With luck, he had simply put some distance between Adianna and this house. With less luck, she was somewhere in Europe, trying to find a phone to call Dominique to arrange a plane home.

CHAPTER 20

"NOW WHAT?" Sarah asked.

"No fight, Sarah? No bold words?" he asked, stepping toward her. "Are your knives all that give you courage?"

"My knives are necessary for me to kill your kind," she answered. "But they aren't my courage. I'm not begging for my life, either."

"You never will, will you?" he asked, as he took hold of her right arm. He bent his head down to the rose and licked away the thin line of blood that had gathered on the stem. Then his lips moved to her throat.

Once again she started to pull away, but

this time she had no knives to threaten with, and Nikolas's grip was tightening. His fangs brushed across her throat and she braced herself for pain.

He raised his head to look her in the eye.

"It doesn't hurt, Sarah," he said, as if reading her mind. "And I'm not going to kill you. What are you afraid of?"

The unknown, Sarah thought. What exactly did this creature have planned? But she didn't ask, because she didn't really want to know. "Just get on with it."

With his free hand he leaned her head back, his fingers running through her hair, strangely gentle.

"Nikolas, let her go."

Nikolas raised his head, allowing Sarah just enough room to look to the speaker.

"Christopher." Nikolas's eyes lit up as he whispered his brother's name. "Care to join me?"

"Let her go, or I will take her from you," Christopher ordered, his voice unwavering.

"You can't," Nikolas answered. "You *could,* physically—you know I wouldn't fight you—but you can't by law." Nikolas gestured to the thin line of blood on his side where Adianna's knife had pierced the skin. "Her sister drew blood. I have claim on Adianna and her relations."

Blood claim was one of the few laws vampires regularly followed. In return for the blood Adianna had drawn from Nikolas, no other vampire was allowed to interfere if he wanted to harm her or anyone in her family.

Christopher closed his eyes for a moment, taking a deep breath. "Don't hurt her."

"Whoever said I was going to hurt her?" He sounded so innocent, it made Sarah nervous.

"I *know* you, Nikolas," Christopher argued.

"Once you did," Nikolas said quietly, sadly. "We—not I, but *we*—were the most feared of our kind. Rome, Paris, New York—every city in the world was ours. What happened to Kristopher and Nikolas, who would hunt side by side, sharing the blood, dancing in the streets?"

Nikolas gestured to the wounds on Sarah's arms. "These marks were *ours*, not mine, and everyone knew it. Now, even the hunters have forgotten you. When was the last time I saw you place your mark on your prey?"

"Marguerite," Christopher answered, lost in memory. He stepped forward until he was standing in front of his brother. "She was the last."

"Why?" Nikolas asked, voice barely audible.

"Let it go, Nikolas," Christopher ordered, his voice shaking slightly. "That was fifty years ago."

"I can see it in your eyes, Christopher," Nikolas whispered to his brother. "You remember. Why did you leave me?"

"I stopped killing, Nikolas—"

"You stopped living!" Nikolas shouted, his emotion breaking any control he had. "I look at you, and all I see is pain. For you I tried to survive on anything but the blood of humans, but I couldn't stand the pain. I couldn't walk in the sunlight. I couldn't stand to be near humans. One day I ran into a human girl on the street, and before I knew it she was dead in my arms. An *innocent human girl,* Christopher, who didn't deserve to die."

Sarah's confusion escalated. Since when did Nikolas care if his victims were innocent or not?

"You were always stronger," Nikolas finished. "I don't have your control."

Christopher looked anything but strong. Sarah could see the bloodlust close to the surface. She was still trapped in Nikolas's arms, and her wounds had opened enough for blood to bead around the edges. The scent of her witch blood was in the air, laced with power and a hint of danger.

"Why did you leave me, Christopher?" Nikolas asked as he reached around Sarah to take his brother's hands. She was trapped between the two vampires, and not sure how to react. Christopher's control was obviously slipping—if she fought now, she would destroy it altogether. She did not want Christopher's life to be the price of her escape.

"You remember Marguerite," Nikolas said. "She picked *us*. She knew what we were and what she wanted—"

"She said she wanted to die," Christopher whispered. The memory was so strong in his voice that Sarah could almost imagine the scene, and the vision caused her to pull at Nikolas's grip for a moment before she forced herself to stop.

Christopher's control was so thin. If he

could contain the bloodlust long enough to get his brother to let her go, she would be grateful. If he lost it, she would fight.

It no longer mattered who was speaking as they continued the tale, both lost in memory. "Two of us, like a mirror. We both fed on her, you on the left, and me on the right. You marked her first, putting your signature forever on her skin, and then I followed."

"And when she woke she was afraid, but there was passion there too. She was given the finest wines and the softest silks to wear, rich foods, chocolates—"

"We approached her again, both of us taking her blood, but this time we only took a taste—"

"And then we both cut ourselves, here, just below our throats, and she leaned forward to drink."

Disgust flashed in Sarah's mind, as she weighed the brothers' every word for a hint of what their next action would be. So the girl had wanted to die. Instead they had blood bonded her, given her all but immortality.

Nikolas drew his brother forward, and

then placed Christopher's hand over the un-cut skin on Sarah's left wrist.

"Why is there nothing here, Christopher?"

Both of the brothers seemed entranced by their pasts. Finally, Sarah spoke.

"You said you haven't hunted since Mar-guerite, Christopher," she said, loudly, in an attempt to break the spell. "Why?"

Christopher blinked and looked at Sarah as if he were seeing her for the first time.

"Nissa took him away from me," Nikolas answered sullenly.

"Nissa needed me," Christopher answered tiredly. "You saw how she was, Nikolas. She hadn't fed in a week. If I hadn't—"

Nikolas's voice was quiet as he inter-rupted. "Don't you know how lonely it is hunting without you?"

"No," Christopher answered, still looking at his brother. "I don't. I've never hunted alone."

Nikolas once again drew his brother for-ward, this time placing Christopher's hand just above the pulse on Sarah's throat. She checked her reaction to jerk back, knowing that an attempt to flee would only bring out the predatory instincts that Christopher was fighting.

"Can't you feel the life there, Christopher?" Nikolas pressed. "Don't you want it?"

Christopher closed his eyes, turning his head away.

"Christopher—"

"Sarah, don't talk," Christopher said quickly, sounding pained. He jerked his hand out of Nikolas's grasp and stepped back.

"Christopher, don't leave me again," Nikolas pleaded, childlike in his fear of loneliness. "I don't want to be alone anymore. Nissa needed you then, but I need you *now*."

"Let Sarah go." Christopher's voice wavered.

"She *hurt* you," Nikolas argued. "I *saw* you after she turned you away. You wouldn't even talk to me. I can't stand to see you in pain, Christopher. In the old days we would have hunted her down together."

"I don't want to kill her," Christopher said. He finally gathered the strength to meet his brother's gaze again. "And I won't let you."

"I won't kill her if you don't want me to — if I was willing to do that she would have been dead the instant she entered my home. But you know I can't just turn her loose. She hunted me down once. Do you really think she would stay away if I let her go? Do you really think her family wouldn't track down you and Nissa if they couldn't find me?" Nikolas's voice was cold, but filled with pain.

"Nikolas—"

Nikolas removed his knife from his pocket and opened it.

"Nikolas, what are you doing?" Christopher demanded, but his brother did not answer as he caught Sarah's right wrist in a grip she could not break, and skimmed the blade across the back of her hand, drawing a thin line of new blood.

"Damn it, Nikolas!" Christopher shouted, spinning sharply away so the blood was not in his sight. "Don't do this to me!"

"Just once, Brother, be the Kristopher I know."

Christopher was trembling as he fought the bloodlust.

"Please, Brother. For me, kill the pain." Holding Sarah by the throat with one hand, Nikolas reached out and turned his brother around with the other. Christopher's eyes

immediately fell on the blood that was drip-
ping from Sarah's hand.

"Christopher, no—"

"*Shut up*, Sarah!" Christopher shouted
when she tried to argue, his voice strained.
He turned to his brother. "We're both
damned. You know that, don't you?"

And then Christopher took Sarah's hand,
lifted the wound to his lips, and licked the
blood away.

"Christopher, I'm your friend—"

"No, Nikolas." Roughly, Christopher
shoved himself away from her, sending
Sarah stumbling back into Nikolas. She
could see him shaking from the effort it took
him to break away.

"Kristopher, have you forgotten everything?" Nikolas pleaded, the hurt clear in his
voice.

"Please, Nikolas, let her go."

"Why?" Nikolas's voice was childlike,
hurt. "You were the first one," he reminded
his brother, "to pick up a knife."

Sarah felt Nikolas's hold on her wrists
lessen as he focused on his brother; if he continued to be distracted, she stood a chance of

getting out. She had lost hope that Christopher would help her—he wasn't strong
enough to ignore his bloodlust.

"Please, Kristopher," Nikolas implored.

"Not Sarah."

That last, painful argument almost caused
her to hesitate, but even as she yanked her
arms out of Nikolas's grip she had made her
decision. Survival. She threw herself forward, and before either vampire could react,
she had pinned Christopher to the floor, a
hand over his throat.

"Sarah—"

He didn't have another chance to speak
before she violently dragged at Christopher's
power with her own. He gasped, unable to
fight back, and she winced at the pain she
knew her magic caused him.

There were nine energy centers in the
body, called chakras, that witches could use
to manipulate the energies of another, usually in order to heal. Her line had learned another way to use them, one no witch would
ever use on another mortal creature: to in-
flict pain, and to kill.

It was a desperate move. Any vampire

strong enough to control his own power could reach along the line she had opened and attack her, and she would have no defenses.

But Christopher had not fed on humans for too long. He was powerless against the deadliest of her attacks.

Nikolas froze when he heard his brother scream. Sarah saw him hesitate as he tried to figure out what she had done.

"Let me go, Nikolas," Sarah demanded. "Call that girl back down and tell her to get my knives *now*, or I will drain every drop of power from your brother's body."

"You wouldn't," Nikolas answered softly, a small amount of fear in his voice.

"He just licked blood off my hand," she growled. "That gives me the motivation to cause some exceptional *pain* if you do not give me back what is mine and let me out of here." She didn't want to kill Christopher. She didn't even want to hurt him. But the choice was between letting him go and having Nikolas kill her, and hurting him and living through this night.

Nikolas stepped forward and she once again reached into Christopher's power and *twisted* what she found there.

He shouted out in pain and Nikolas winced, stopping.

"I can kill him in less than a second if you make another move toward me," she warned, and it was true. As entrenched in Christopher's power as she was, she could tear, tangle, or destroy with a thought.

"Marguerite, get the knives," Nikolas whispered, and the human who had been watching from the doorway ran upstairs. Sarah had seen the fear on the girl's face—fear for Christopher's life, for the vampire who had fed on her years ago when she wanted to die, and then given her this life in exchange for the one she had abandoned.

Nikolas took a step back, but Sarah could see pure hatred smoldering in his eyes as he did so.

Marguerite returned and held Sarah's knives out to her. Keeping her right hand over Christopher's throat, she returned all the knives to their rightful places with her left. Still holding Christopher by the throat, she stood.

"I am going to let him go, and you are going to leave me alone. Do we have a deal, Nikolas?"

"I'm going to kill you the first chance I get," he growled back, and Christopher once again shouted out in pain.

"Do we have a deal, Nikolas?"

"For tonight, I will let you leave safely," he answered.

"Agreed," she said, as she relaxed her hold on Christopher, who collapsed to the floor. "He's going to die if he doesn't feed soon, Nikolas," she warned before he had a chance to make a move.

Without hesitation Nikolas drew Christopher to his own throat.

CHAPTER 21

"WHAT IN THE WORLD did you think you were doing?" Adianna demanded the instant Sarah entered the house.

Sarah pushed past her sister without answering. She was too tired to deal with questions tonight.

Adianna followed in silence, waiting to speak until they were almost in Sarah's room. "You aren't invincible, Sarah, and you well know it. Yet you're always throwing yourself into these situations, going alone where no hunter in her right mind would—"

"I couldn't bring you," Sarah interrupted

tiredly. "I can't explain, but it wasn't just because I like doing things alone."

"You don't have to protect me," Adianna
stated.

"This time I did. This is something between Nikolas and me."

"No, it's *not*," Adianna argued. "You are a
Daughter of Vida, Sarah. A witch. A hunter.
He marked you, and for that you are seeking
vengeance. But that is *not* what you are here
for. You are here to protect the humans who
cannot protect themselves. Not to get yourself killed for a personal insult."

"I've heard the lecture before," Sarah
snapped, her frayed nerves ruining the last
of her patience. "Now, please, leave me
alone."

"You're acting suicidal, Sarah."

"Good night, Adianna." Sarah slipped into
her room and closed the door on her sister.
Adianna knocked a couple of times, but finally gave up and let Sarah alone.

Nissa was the one she was worried about.
The girl didn't take human blood meals, but
if the other hunters learned Nikolas was her
relation, she would never be able to rest

safely. The last thing Sarah wanted was for hunters to push Nissa into killing to defend herself.

Christopher . . . what was she going to do about Christopher? She might have just helped Nikolas convince his brother to start killing again, but it was what she had needed to do to survive.

It wasn't her fault. She had never asked for any of this. She had never asked for anything more complex than the simple definitions of good and evil she had been raised on.

All she could think was that she was marked, that Nikolas had signed his name on her skin as if she were some kind of object, and now he was hunting her. All to defend his brother. Wouldn't she have done the same—worse, actually—to someone who had hurt Adianna?

She shook her head violently, trying to let go of these dangerous thoughts, and threw herself down on the bed, hoping for a sleep that eluded her.

She would kill him.

If she could.

If she could turn her heart into stone and

make her knife her only morals, if she could stand to kill Christopher and Nissa when they came to avenge Nikolas's death, if she could stand living after killing her friends, then she would kill Nikolas.

CHAPTER 22

SARAH INTERCEPTED ROBERT by his car at the end of the next school day.

"What's up?"

She was aware that she looked very different than when they had last spoken. Her black jeans and white shirt were plain, not exactly her style, but she wore them because she planned on visiting someone who wasn't fond of colors. Her leather jacket covered her arms. She had not bothered to replace the bandages after last night. Her blond hair was down, slightly wild, stirred up by her running to the parking lot. Her eyes smoldered with intensity and purpose.

"I need to talk to your sister."

"Not likely. I told you already, Kristin doesn't talk to anyone. She barely even *sees* anyone anymore."

Sarah leaned back against his car door, and repeated herself. "I need to talk to Kristin, and I'm pretty sure she'll talk to me."

He snorted. "I'm not bringing you to her. If she notices you at all, she'll just freak out."

"Robert—"

"Leave me alone, okay?" he snapped. "I get it. I'm not as . . . important . . . as you are. I'm human, yeah, fine. I talked to your mother, and she made that quite clear. Now leave me alone."

"No," she answered calmly. She felt a little guilty about sending this human to her mother, but he had received no colder welcome than any other hunter had. "I need to talk to Kristin, and I thought it would be more polite to ask than to break into your house."

This time he tried to muscle past her, pushing her to the side. He was bigger than she was, but he hadn't counted on her strength; his shove didn't even knock her off balance.

"Robert . . . , " she said, trailing off. There was only one way to get his attention.

Show-and-tell. She shrugged off the leather jacket and watched Robert's eyes widen at the sight of her fresh wounds. "I know a lot more about him than you do. I've fought him twice, and I know he plans to try to kill me soon. I need to know what Kristin knows, and if she knows some way to hurt him."

Robert hesitated, then stepped back reluctantly. "Fine." He got in his side of the car and reached over to unlock the passenger-side door. "I can't guarantee she'll talk to you, but if you think she can help you get that monster . . ." He trailed off. "Get in the car."

CHAPTER 23

THOUGH THERE WAS COLOR in it, Robert's house seemed bleached of life.

"Kristin's room is upstairs," Robert said quietly, and led Sarah up the blue-gray carpeted stairs. Just outside his sister's door, he spoke again. "If you can help her, or get her to help you, fine. But Kristin . . . isn't all there. She probably won't even notice you. Don't bully her—she doesn't need any more abuse."

Kristin was dressed in a long white nightgown with a high collar. Her hair had been dyed black, though the natural brown showed for about an inch at the roots.

The room was devoid of even gray — black paint covered every spot that might have been colored, and flaked off the handle of the hairbrush Kristin was using.

Nikolas's house had been just as colorless, but that had been neat, artistic somehow — this was just sick.

"Kristin, I need to talk to you." The girl didn't look up, but continued brushing her hair. "Kristin?" Still there was no reaction from the girl. "I need to talk to you about Nikolas."

The brush paused.

"Kristin . . ." The girl returned to brushing her hair, and Sarah sighed.

Sarah knelt, moving the marks on her arms into Kristin's line of sight, and finally the girl looked at her.

"*He* sent you?" she asked, and the hope in her eyes was strong.

There was pain in Sarah's voice as she answered, "No. But I need to talk to you about him."

"I . . . I don't know much. It was only one party—"

"Just tell me what happened there."

"I don't—" She looked at her brother and

shivered as her eyes fell on his washed-out blue shirt; he took it off, throwing it from the room.

"Better, Kristin?"

She nodded slowly and Robert left to get a different shirt.

"This girl Heather invited me to the party. She said the people were cool, and the music was awesome, and the guy she was going with was completely hot . . . which was strange, 'cause Heather is so cold, not really caring about anything . . ."

Sarah choked back her revulsion. The Heather whom Kristin was talking about was probably the one Sarah had seen at Nikolas's bash, asking Kaleo to bite her. What kind of human invited other, defenseless humans into that kind of place?

Kristin had trailed off. "Tell me about the party," Sarah prompted, and Kristin nodded.

"The house . . . there was so much color in it, like walking into a kaleidoscope . . . one room was all red . . . it scared me . . ."

"Was Nikolas there?"

"The people . . . it was strange, the groups. Some of them were like me. They didn't seem to know what was going on, really, and the house unnerved them a bit. Others were like Heather. They had connections. And others, so detached, so . . ." She shook her head, unable to find the description she was looking for.

"And then there was *him,* Nikolas . . .

"He was so beautiful, completely in contrast with everything else . . . his skin was so pale, and he was wearing all black . . . beautiful. He asked me my name and I told him it was Christine . . . he didn't like that. He didn't say anything, but I could tell."

Christine . . . did she remind Nikolas of the Christine who had hurt his brother? Had some slight nuance of expression been so important that the girl now refused to respond to her real name?

"But he asked me to dance, and I thought I might just *die,* because he was *so* handsome and . . . unearthly. I'd say like an angel but he wasn't at all, he was like . . . I don't know . . . seductive, just by *existing.*"

Kristin sighed, then continued. "After the dance he held me in his arms a minute longer, and I remember . . . I remember his lips on my throat and I just *relaxed,* because it felt so good . . ." She gestured to the marks on her arms. "I don't remember when he made these . . . they didn't hurt . . ." She paused.

"And then?" Sarah said, and the girl blinked.

"No, I don't want to talk anymore."

"You started telling us, Kristin—you have to finish," Sarah said, meeting her eyes. She wasn't as good as the vampires at influencing human minds, but Kristin's defenses were weak.

Kristin nodded. "He . . . he didn't really take much blood. I remember not wanting him to stop when he pulled away, because it felt so good . . ."

Robert made a sickened sound, but Kristin didn't notice as she went on. "And he said . . . he said, 'I want to make you mine.' And I said yes and yes was all I could say for a moment, but then I said no." She shook her head, trying to clear it. "And he . . . he looked so *surprised*, and he just asked why . . . and I . . . I said, 'Because I need to go home,' and he asked why again, and I said, 'Because my brother will be sad if I don't go home, and he'll be lonely.' "

She put her head into her hands and

started to cry. "And he . . . he pushed me away and said, 'Get out,' and that's all he would say to me. I didn't understand and I tried to talk to him, but he pulled some other person over and said, 'Get her out of here.' "

"And then?"

"Then . . . the other guy asked, 'And do what with her?' and Nikolas said, he said, 'I don't care, just get her home to her brother.' And . . . no."

"Go on, Kristin," Sarah urged, but the girl just shook her head.

"No, no . . ."

Despite Sarah's encouragement, Kristin would say no more. The block was partially vampiric mind control, but mostly simple, human denial.

CHAPTER 24

ALL THREE OF THEM jumped at the knock on the door.

"Who is it?" Robert called.

"Is Sarah in there? It's Nissa—I need to talk to her—"

Robert had opened the door before Sarah could tell him otherwise. Sarah fell back into a fighting stance, unsure what Nissa wanted.

"Sarah, I'm glad I tracked you down. Nikolas is calling for your blood. What the hell did you do to Christopher?"

"I did what I needed to do to survive," Sarah answered, but Nissa's attention had left her and moved onto Kristin, who was huddled in a corner, sobbing.

"God . . ." Nissa looked at the marks on Kristin's arms, and then said, "Nikolas didn't do this to her. These are his marks, but he would never . . . leave someone like this."

Robert frowned. "If he didn't, who did?"

"What are you doing here?" Nissa asked, as if just realizing that the human boy was in the room.

"I live here," he answered. "And since you're in my house, maybe you should answer my questions."

Nissa just shook her head. "What happened to her?"

"Why do you care?"

"Why do I care?" Nissa said between her teeth. "I care because she is a living human being, and she's . . ." She shook her head violently, and then put a hand on Kristin's shoulder. The girl looked up at Nissa, who caught her eye.

Kristin screamed again, bolting from Nissa's hold.

"What the hell did you do to her?" Robert demanded.

"I just tried to find the memories of what caused . . . *that*," Nissa spat, looking at Kristin. "I should have known this is the kind of mess Kaleo would leave behind."

"*Kaleo?*" Robert repeated. "Who the hell is Kaleo?"

Nissa laughed, a pained sound, but she did not answer. Instead, she turned back to Kristin, who was sitting silently in the corner, terrified. "I don't think I can help her. Kaleo has her blood bonded to himself, and I'm not strong enough to reach her mind through that."

"You mean someone stronger could help her?" Robert asked, catching the unspoken statement.

"I don't know exactly what *caused* this, but if someone could reach her mind through all the mess he's put in there, they could help."

Robert stalked over to where Nissa was standing. "I don't want to know what you are or what relation to Nikolas you have. If you can help my sister, or get someone who can, I don't care if you're the devil herself."

Nissa shook her head. "I don't think—"

"Please. If you know how to help her, you have to. She wasn't like this before. She was . . . colorful. Alive. Intelligent. Kind. She had dreams. But the monster who did this took all that away."

"I know someone who would be strong enough to help her," Nissa said slowly, but she looked over Robert's shoulder and met Sarah's gaze. "But he—"

"Then get him to do it!" Robert ordered, but Sarah was very slowly shaking her head.

"Sarah?" Nissa left the rest of the question unspoken.

"Would he help?" Sarah asked quietly. "Or would he do more damage than Kaleo did?"

"I think he would help," Nissa answered, and Sarah nodded.

"Fine, then." She was leaving sanity in the hands of the insane. Since when were the monsters called in to heal the innocent?

Nissa disappeared, and Robert shouted, "That . . . that . . ."

"Was one of the simplest vampire tricks you will ever see. She could be in China now with no more effort than you would use to blink."

Robert sat down, his legs folding under him.

"Is she gone?" Kristin whispered as she lifted her head.

"For the moment," Robert answered, still dazed.

While Nissa was gone, Sarah drew the knife from the sheath on her back, unsure what was going to happen once she reappeared.

"What's that for?" Robert asked, nervous.

"Just in case I need it," she answered. She moved so her back was to a wall, and crossed her arms. She could defend herself if necessary, but she didn't want to start a fight if Nikolas was going to help Kristin.

"You just carry that thing around?"

"This and two others," Sarah answered. "Sometimes more. It depends whether the knife sheaths match my outfit."

Robert looked at her as if she might be crazy, but then seemed to realize she was making a joke. He *didn't* realize that she was also telling the complete truth—she tried to wear as many knives as her outfit would safely hide.

Then Nissa reappeared with Nikolas and everything happened at once.

Robert's eyes narrowed as he realized who Nikolas must be—*black and white*.

Sarah and Nikolas locked glares, and he took a step toward her.

Nissa stepped between Nikolas and Sarah.

Kristin vaulted across the room and fell at Nikolas's feet.

Nikolas's attention snapped away from Sarah as he pulled Kristin up, looking at her quizzically. Sarah could see recognition in his eyes.

"Christine," he recalled aloud.

The girl did not argue the name, but instead nodded, leaning against him. Nikolas tensed for a moment, and then put a comforting arm around her, looking over her to where Robert was standing.

"You're the brother?" Robert nodded. "I sent Christine home. What happened to her?"

Robert opened his mouth, closed it, opened it again. "I thought . . ."

"She told us what happened up until you sent her off," Sarah said. "Then she broke down, hysterical. Nissa said Kaleo did this." *Since when did Nikolas turn into a cuddly sweetheart?* Sarah wondered cynically, seeing the tenderness with which Nikolas held Kristin.

Nikolas's eyes narrowed. "It would be like him." He looked around the room, taking in the lack of color, perhaps seeing even more in it than Sarah had. "This isn't his, though . . . Kaleo likes color, especially red."

Kristin shivered, and put her head down on Nikolas's chest, crying.

"She can't stand color anymore," Robert explained, watching his sister in Nikolas's gentle embrace. "She screams at anything red."

Nikolas nodded, and then returned his attention to Kristin, lifting her face.

"What happened after I sent you away, Christine?"

She shook her head violently. "No, no—"

"Christine, look at me!" Nikolas ordered. He put his hands on her shoulders and forced her to meet his gaze. Sarah heard the echo of his voice in her own mind, and she could tell that Nikolas was forcing his words into Kristin's mind as he spoke aloud. *You're . . . safe, Christine. No one is going to hurt you. Calm down.*

Kristin relaxed a bit as his mind reached into hers, speaking his words directly to her thoughts.

Now tell me what happened.

"No, I—" She broke off, finally looking away from his black eyes. "You sent me away, and he took me outside . . . he said you didn't care what happened to me . . ."

"Go on."

"And he . . . he bit me, but it wasn't like when you bit me, it *hurt* . . ." She moaned. "I tried to push him away but it just hurt more . . ."

She collapsed back into sobs and he put his arms around her, comforting. He ran his fingers through her hair, and Sarah saw him hesitate when he noticed the dye.

"Go on, Christine. He isn't here; it doesn't hurt anymore."

"I think I blacked out, and when I woke up I was in a hospital, and people were asking me questions, about *you*. That's all they cared about. The police thought you had hurt me, and I told them no, you tried to send me home, but no one would believe me. And they had an IV in me, and the blood was so red . . ."

She was babbling now, but Nikolas simply held her, looking over her shoulder as if he couldn't stand to see the mess she had become.

"Christine," he said, looking her in the eye. "It's over now —"

"No!" She screamed it. "They keep telling me it's *over* . . . that there's nothing to be afraid of, that . . . but it *isn't* . . . it *isn't* . . ."

Now she did collapse, and Nikolas caught her easily. He whispered into her ear and she moaned in unconsciousness. Suddenly his eyes narrowed as he found something in her mind he didn't like.

"I'll kill him, Christine," he said softly, speaking to the unconscious girl. "I wasn't strong enough to protect Father, but for this, Kaleo is dead." Looking up, he spoke to Robert. "I'm taking her with me."

"Like hell you are!" Robert started to lunge at Nikolas, but Nikolas pulled his knife from his pocket and snapped it open, tilting it toward Robert.

"You don't understand, boy. Kaleo has been feeding on her—not just once, but ever since he found her," Nikolas snapped. "And he has blood bonded her to himself, which means he has complete control over her mind. I'm taking her someplace safe until I can stop him. Then, if she wants to return, I'll bring her back."

"Like I would believe you."

"I never lie," Nikolas answered, and

Robert glared at him. "Normally, the humans invited to our circuit are loners—they don't have anyone to miss them, or anyone to miss. Christine should never have been invited in the first place. Once I am satisfied she is safe, I will let her come home. I would not take her away from her brother."

Robert was unconvinced. "Let go of my sister."

"I was asked to help her—do you really want me to leave her here until Kaleo drives her completely insane?" Robert took a step back, but his glare didn't soften. Nikolas sighed. "Did she ever once say I hurt her?"

"You knifed her!" Robert shouted.

"I *marked* her. That should have protected her from Kaleo. But I told him I didn't care what happened to her, so long as she got home. Did she ever say I *hurt* her?"

"What are you trying to prove?" Robert demanded.

"I do not torture my prey the way Kaleo does." Sarah smirked, and Nikolas commented, "As I recall, Sarah, you were trying to kill me. You're a Daughter of Vida, and you broke into my home. I would hardly consider you prey."

"You don't torture your prey," Sarah challenged. "You just kill them."

Nikolas shrugged, acknowledging the truth. "Yes, I kill. I have no reason to deny that fact." Turning to Robert, he said, "But I will not kill Christine." He whispered something else, and Sarah thought she might have heard him say *"Again."*

"Just for the record, what happens once you're satisfied she's safe?" Sarah asked.

Nikolas looked up and then tossed something in her direction. She caught it instinctively, and Nikolas disappeared, taking Kristin with him.

CHAPTER 25

SARAH CAUGHT NISSA'S ARM before the other girl could disappear, and herded her into another room.

"What is he up to?" she demanded instantly.

Nissa looked startled. "What?"

"Nikolas is a self-admitted killer. Suddenly he's all heart."

Nissa shook her head slowly. "Nikolas is . . . Nikolas," she answered vaguely. "His marks make him more blatant among vampire hunters, but he isn't even as bad as most of my kind." She sighed. "You see him only as a killer, the same way he sees you only as a threat to himself and Christopher. Nikolas has rules of his own, and he would never torment an innocent girl like Christine.

"Nikolas sees you as his enemy because you threatened someone he cares about." Nissa sighed, grasping for the words. "But Christine is someone he has chosen to defend. Nikolas is a harsh enemy, but much of that is because he is a fierce protector."

Sarah shook her head, not understanding. "So he chooses to protect Christine . . . but at the next bash, or probably even tonight when he hunts, he will kill some other girl who might as well be her."

Nissa looked heavenward as if for assistance, which was not forthcoming. "You know my brothers used to hunt together. They had—and Nikolas still has—scores of admirers, all of whom were completely safe. They were more than willing to donate blood, and beyond them, people would come to my brothers who wanted to die. I will never understand how my brothers' minds work, but they aren't . . . evil. They could never be that."

Robert entered the room and Sarah jumped at the sudden intrusion.

He turned to Nissa. "Is my sister going to be safe with this guy?" he demanded.

Nissa nodded. "With Nikolas is probably the safest place she could ever be."

Robert nodded sharply. Then he groaned, and leaned back against the wall. "What the hell am I going to tell my parents?" He turned back to Nissa. "Never mind. I don't care about my parents. Thank you. Tell Nikolas that too. I just want my sister to get better."

Nissa smiled faintly. "I'll tell him, the next time I see him."

She disappeared, and Sarah finally relaxed. Remembering the note she was still holding, she quickly skimmed over the words.

Cold as winter, strong as stone;
She faced the darkness all alone.
A silver goddess; a reflection.
A mirage; a recollection.
No return; no turning back.
The past is gone, the future, black.
Serpents gather in their nest,
And she stands above the rest.
Shadows hunt; she hunts the shadow.

The moon is risen; she stands below.
She views her world through the eyes of
others.
Black and white; there are no colors,
As she looks down upon a shattered youth.
A shattered mirror shows a shattered truth.

The poem reminded her of the notes Christopher sent to her.

On the back of the paper was a drawing of Nikolas, standing back to back with Christopher . . . or a reflection of himself. At the bottom of the paper were three words, written in black ink: *Midnight; my house.*

"I don't think so," she whispered.

Robert looked over at her shoulder and read the message. "You going?"

"I already gave him a free shot at me. I'm not really suicidal," she answered absently.

"Huh?"

"He said he would help your sister," Sarah snapped. "That doesn't mean he's suddenly a good guy. He isn't particularly fond of me, and if I go there, he will try to kill me."

"He didn't act like he wanted to kill you," Robert pointed out. "And what's this poetry about—"

"Robert, give it up!"

"I think you're misunderstanding some-thing—"

"Robert, I'm a vampire hunter. Nikolas is a vampire. He has a million and one reasons to kill me and not one to let me live. Don't let poetry and a moment of kindness on his part fool you. Nikolas has only one way of deal-ing with things, and that's by killing. You heard it when he was talking about Kaleo."

"The guy who did that to my sister deserves to die," Robert growled. "I'd kill him too."

"I'll deal with Kaleo later. The only one on my hit list right now is Nikolas."

"No," Robert said.

"What?"

"No," he repeated. "If you kill Nikolas, what's going to happen to Christine?" he de-manded. "Kaleo will keep hurting her, and—"

"Doesn't anyone remember that Nikolas is a killer?" she hissed.

Sarah cut off his answer and left abruptly. Robert didn't understand, and she didn't know how to explain to him. Instead she went home and collapsed onto her bed, still holding Nikolas's invitation.

CHAPTER 26

SARAH RETURNED to wakefulness gasping, struggling to fill lungs with air thick as charcoal ashes, and struggling to clear vision fogged with . . . she didn't know. She could see, but the sight seemed imperfect and she could not tell why.

"Sarah Tigress Vida, stand up."

Her mother's voice, formal and cold, instantly cleared Sarah's mind despite the disorientation she could not seem to shake. She felt off-balance as she found her feet, trying to keep herself from shaking. She sought uselessly to smooth her wrinkled jeans.

Adianna stood behind Dominique, her

face pained as she sought Sarah's gaze. Sarah opened her mouth to speak, but Dominique cut her off before she could say a word.

"I want no excuses," Dominique stated flatly. "I am not a fool, and I have known what has been going on since the start of these events." At these words, Adianna's gaze fell. "You were warned, and you had more than one chance to halt this . . . disgusting infatuation. Now this." Dominique threw to the ground Nikolas's poem-invitation.

"Mother—"

Dominique held up a hand to halt her daughter's words. "I might have turned a blind eye upon your association with the vampires at your school, since you would have in time come to your senses, but *this* . . . lying about this killer, *protecting* him," Dominique spat, "this I can not forgive."

Succinctly and in order, Sarah's crimes were listed. Befriending her prey. Lying to her kin. Endangering her kind by revealing them to the vampires when she told Christopher the truth. Bargaining with Nikolas, and giving up her Vida knife. Telling the human Robert who she was without Dominique's

permission. The list went on and on, including transgressions so minor they would have
been overlooked any other time, and through
it all Sarah had no choice but to try to stand
without swaying.

Sarah reached for her power to steady her
nerves, but found herself grasping at air. She
could feel the magic still humming deep in
her blood, but Dominique had bound it—
that explained the disorientation she had felt
when she had first awakened, and that was
why every sense seemed dulled. Without
her magic available, she was little more than
human.

"You have until tomorrow night to prepare yourself," Dominique announced at
last.

To prepare herself for the trial, Sarah
knew. By then Dominique would have gathered the leaders of the other lines, and Sarah
doubted she would be acquitted. Every word
Dominique had spoken had been true.

When Dominique turned and left the
room, Sarah sank back onto the bed, dazed.
Again she tried to reach for her power; she
could sense it so clearly, but could not use it.

What would it feel like to have it stripped away completely?

It was only eight o'clock at night. So early, but it might as well have been the end of the world.

"Sarah . . ." Adianna's voice was soft as she closed the door and sat beside her sister. "I'm sorry. I thought you had the sense to break it off with them, and I thought you would be better off if Dominique knew right away rather than finding out sometime later . . ." Adianna shook her head. "I never should have let it get this far."

Sarah's eyes widened as Adianna quietly ordered, "Get out of here. As it is, your magic will come back in a few days, and you still have your knife. But if you're here to-morrow night, Dominique will disown you and take it all away."

"I'm not going to hide from her."

Adianna shook her head violently. "This isn't about your pride anymore, Sarah. This is about your *life*—"

"And when Dominique asks where I've gone? Will you lie for me?" Sarah demanded. "I won't have you killed for me."

"I won't be," Adianna answered calmly. "Besides Dominique herself, no one will fault me for defending my sister." When she saw Sarah's hesitation, she added, "It's your only choice, Sarah."

"To hide for the rest of my life from every one of my kind doesn't seem like a very good choice."

Adianna swallowed thickly. "Better than being dead." Her gaze still locked on Sarah's, she stood up and turned away. "I'm going to bed, Sarah. I'm going to lock my door and turn on loud music, and if I don't hear a car leaving, that's not my fault." She shrugged. "Good night."

After Adianna closed the door, Sarah sat for a moment more.

To hide forever was not a very good option. Neither was being disowned—and she had no hope that she would be found innocent of the crimes Dominique had listed.

Her gaze fell on the invitation Dominique had thrown to the ground, and her decision was made. There was only one way out.

She spent about an hour orientating herself, getting used to using her body without the sixth sense her magic usually provided, and she was confident she could do what she needed to.

She needed to kill Nikolas.

Sarah wrote a note to Adianna and Dominique, stating her intent. Dominique had accused her of endangering her kin and protecting Nikolas—which, in her attempt to protect Nissa and Christopher, she had done. The only possible way out of this mess was to confront Nikolas.

In truth, Nikolas wasn't the worst of his kind—he didn't torture his prey, and he didn't kill nearly so wantonly as his strength would allow. He hunted, as all vampires hunted, to kill the bloodlust. His marks were the only element that made his kills more obvious than kills by others of his kind. Had Christopher not separated from his brother before Dominique had started organizing the chaotic mess her predecessors had allowed the Vida records to become, his marks and name would have been just as infamous as his brother's.

This was not the time to ponder Christopher's guilt or Nikolas's innocence. This was the reason hunters knew better than to mix with their prey. It created shades of gray, where there had once been just black and white.

She didn't know what she would do when Nissa and Christopher hunted her down. She refused to kill them. But she also refused to run; hiding until she died, old and lonely, seemed worse by far than dying the quick death every hunter knew marked the end.

She didn't bother to hide her knives when she left, but instead put on a black tank top and black shorts; over everything she threw her leather jacket, so the weapons wouldn't be quite so obvious while she was still in the human world.

After taking the keys to her Jaguar from the dresser, she went outside and started the car.

The clock read 11:59 as she pulled into the driveway at Nikolas's house.

CHAPTER 27

NIKOLAS TOOK HER COAT as she entered. The house was empty except for the two of them.

Three of us, she realized, as Nikolas led her into the living room, where Christopher was pacing.

"Are you losing your resolve, Sarah?" Nikolas asked, and Christopher halted in his pacing. "You've been near enough to kill me for a whole two minutes, and you haven't even drawn a knife."

"Is Christine okay?" Sarah asked, not acknowledging Nikolas's question.

Nikolas sighed. "Christine is fine. Even

Kaleo is still alive. In fact, I haven't had a chance to kill anyone noteworthy in the ten hours since I last spoke with you. Does that settle your curiosity?"

Sarah ignored the taunt. "Christopher, what are you doing here?"

Christopher shrugged. "My brother asked me to come."

He looked much the same physically as he had the last time she had seen him, but there was an energy about him that was different.

Christopher had fed. Though she could read his aura easily enough to know he had not killed, he had obviously taken human blood, probably just after their fight, when his bloodlust had been so overwhelming.

Sarah examined his face for a sign of whether he was going to help her or hurt her, but though his expression showed no anger, it showed no compassion either.

"Can I get you something to drink?" Nikolas offered, and Sarah laughed.

Sure, she thought sarcastically, wondering what vampires served to drink. *A Bloody Mary—shaken, not sliced.*

"What are you up to, Nikolas?" she asked instead.

"I invited you to my home. I can at least be a gracious host before you try to kill me."

He was going to wait for her to move? That could make this a very long evening indeed, because she had been planning to wait for his attack. If she killed Nikolas now, unprovoked, she had no illusions that she would not need to kill Christopher, too.

"I'll have something."

Sarah turned to see a girl no older than sixteen. She was wearing a white cotton dress with silver embroidery, and her skin was fair, but not ghostly. Her hair was dark brown.

"Christine?" Sarah whispered, hardly able to believe it. Could this girl be the same wraith Sarah had seen earlier that day, huddled in a corner? She had obviously been cleaned up, dressed, fed . . . the change was so amazing, it seemed impossible.

"Yes," the girl said lightly. "I never caught your name, though."

"Sarah," she answered. She shook Christine's hand as if this were a normal situation, though it was absurd to be introducing herself to this girl now, in the midst of a den of monsters.

She views her world through the eyes of others./Black and white; there are no colors,/As she looks down upon a shattered youth./A shattered mirror shows a shattered truth.

Sarah had never doubted herself before, but this nymph in white caused her hatred of Nikolas to fade a bit. Christine stood on tiptoe to open a tin that was sitting on the mantel above the fireplace.

"Chocolate?" she offered, but Sarah shook her head.

"No, thank you."

Christine glided out of the room again and Sarah watched her go, entranced.

"Nikolas, what do you want?" Christopher finally asked once Christine was out of sight. He sounded drained, tired. "Why am I here?"

"I wanted to give you a chance, Brother," Nikolas said. He reached into his pocket, pulled something out, and tossed it to Christopher.

For a moment Sarah thought the knife was Nikolas's, but as Christopher snapped it open she realized the handle was black with white inlay, the reverse of Nikolas's—Kristopher's, Sarah assumed, left over from the time when the two brothers still hunted together.

Christopher closed the knife. "A chance to do what?"

"To share this one with me," Nikolas answered, and Sarah realized it might be time to start fighting.

But she didn't move.

"You're going to blood bond her to yourself," Christopher said, knowing how his brother's mind worked. "That's why you didn't kill her when you marked her."

"For you, Brother. You wanted her, but she turned you down, Christopher," Nikolas answered. "Now's your chance to make her yours. To make her ours."

"Like Marguerite," Christopher whispered, understanding. "Nikolas, no. Marguerite wanted it. Sarah doesn't."

"She *hurt* you, Christopher," Nikolas said, pleading. "I *heard* you scream. You told me not to kill her—fine, I won't kill her, but there are very few choices left. I can let her go, in which case her own family is going to kill her, or I can blood bond her to myself."

"I'm not going to help you with this, Nikolas—"

"Fine," he answered, his voice childlike and resigned at the same time.

Sarah stepped back out of Nikolas's line of sight, and saw him turn to keep her in his view.

She went for her knife, and an instant later Nikolas was behind her, with his hand around her throat. She drew the knife from her thigh and flipped it in her hand, driving it into his side.

Nikolas cursed, throwing her away from him, and Sarah landed awkwardly on her knife, slicing open her right palm. A moment later a knife blade was at her throat.

Christopher's.

Christopher had Sarah pinned on the floor, with the blade of his knife against her skin.

"Slice me open, Christopher," she hissed. "If you're really willing, then do it."

Though Christopher didn't let the knife cut her, he pressed the blade harder against her skin. If she moved, she would slit her own throat.

Nikolas recovered and knelt by his brother's side, then reached toward the knife on Sarah's back so he could disarm her. His brother caught his wrist, stopping him, and Nikolas nodded.

Christopher moved his knife away and pulled her to her feet, and then he let her go.

Nikolas followed Sarah with his gaze. "Christopher—"

"I'm not going to kill her for defending herself," Christopher interrupted.

"The Kristopher I used to know—my *brother*—would have killed her as soon as he found out she was a Vida. You've tasted her blood. How can you not want it?"

"I want it," Christopher said softly. "I want it as much as humans want to breathe, but I have control."

Sarah backed away, and noticed that, though Nikolas kept a hawk's gaze on her, Christopher was only watching his brother. When she realized how easy it would be to kill him, bile rose in her throat.

"Come back to me, Kristopher. Hunt with me," Nikolas pleaded. He stepped toward his brother, moving closer to Sarah at the same time—he obviously did not trust her at his brother's back. "Why do you let the bloodlust burn you every night and every day? We need to feed to survive. Would a starving man on the verge of death turn down a dinner because it was chicken and he was a vegetarian? Or would he eat it anyway, because it was all he had that could stop the pain?"

Sarah did not wait for Christopher's answer. Instead, she drew the knife from her wrist. The blade had barely cleared its sheath when Nikolas pounced, sending her to the ground; the breath rushed from her lungs, but she kept her grip on her weapon.

Christopher reacted instantly and grabbed his brother's arm, dragging Nikolas to the side, ignoring Sarah as if she posed no threat. Slaughtering her sense of fair play, Sarah rolled, knocking the momentarily defenseless vampire away. Nikolas cried as her blade touched his skin, and the sound caused Sarah's gut to clench. He looked so much like Christopher—so vulnerable.

She realized that she had hesitated only when Christopher's hand clamped over her wrist, stopping the knife from completing the killing blow. He tightened his grip until she dropped the weapon, and Nikolas tossed her knife away while Christopher dragged her away from his brother.

Most vampires were solitary hunters. Sarah had been trained to take down enemies one by one, but Nikolas and Christopher fought like one entity. When one was in danger, the other reacted.

Self-preservation replaced all loyalty to her friend as Sarah slammed an elbow into Christopher's gut, forcing him to release her, in the same moment that Nikolas knocked her legs from beneath her.

She rolled away from both vampires, drawing her last knife. Breathing heavily, she paused, waiting for one of the vampires to move.

Nikolas edged toward her slowly, and she found her feet, her eyes never straying from him. Her right hand was still bleeding, and she saw his gaze fall to it, and the knife she was holding.

She was watching Nikolas, but it was Christopher who caught her wrist, Christopher who was suddenly restraining her. She had fallen for the same mistake he had, only moments before — she had assumed he would not hurt her unless she attacked him, and so had not been paying attention when he had disappeared from in front of her.

Christopher had lost his reasons for refusing, and all three of them knew it. Sarah's blood was in the air, along with the tension from the fight. Christopher's control was already weak, and now the predator had taken control.

Nikolas reached around Sarah and held her wrists, as Kristopher wrapped an arm around her waist to hold her still.

Sarah gasped as twin sets of fangs pierced her skin, Kristopher on the right and Nikolas on the left. Without her magic she had no further defense, and she collapsed beneath the combined pressure of their minds. With Nikolas and Kristopher still at her throat, she sank to her knees.

Both brothers pulled away after a few moments, and their gazes met for barely a second.

Nikolas turned away first, bent to retrieve Kristopher's knife from where it had fallen, and handed it to his brother.

Kristopher took the knife as if he were in a trance and made a cut just below his own throat.

Sarah turned her head away, but Kristopher forced her to look at him—and at the line of blood that beaded on his skin. They had barely taken any of her blood, but even so she could feel the thirst that always fell on a vampire's prey, and she could not look away.

"No." Her voice was soft, almost frightened.

Kristopher touched his fingers to his own blood and painted her lips with it, forcing her mouth open. She tasted the blood of the damned, and she could not resist.

Leaning her head forward to the cut on his chest, she drank. The blood was sweet and thick and magical, and she wanted it so much—

He pushed her away after a moment, and Nikolas turned her to himself, drawing his blade across his own skin, a mirror wound to Kristopher's.

Once again she drank.

Then Nikolas pushed her away too, and she felt her mind spin downward as the blood entered her system. Blackness finally swallowed her, and she fell into the oblivion of unconsciousness.

CHAPTER 28

ADIANNA HAD HER KNIFE in her hand as she shouldered open the front door, but she already knew there were no vampires within a mile of her. Her senses were stretched so far she could feel the heartbeats of the human inside and those of most of the humans on this block. Worse, she could feel Sarah, her aura muted from Dominique's binding of her powers, and her heart beating frantically.

All this she knew before she even stepped into the front hall of the house. Her eyes took in, but her mind ignored, the artwork, the roses on the table, and the open box of chocolates on the mantel.

More vividly she saw the droplets of deep red blood, not yet dried, but scattered as if from a minor wound on a fighting person.

She should have guessed what Sarah would do. Adianna herself would have done the same, if somehow she had ended up in the same situation. Better to die than to face the humiliation of being disowned. Better to die with your pride intact than to live without it. They had both been raised that way, but Adianna had hoped so fiercely that Sarah would choose life. It had been almost two hours later that she had sneaked back to Sarah's room, only to find her already gone.

Sarah's spilled blood, blond hair, and flushed skin were the only color in the room. She lay on a plush black couch, where it seemed someone had gently set her down. Adianna could see the faint mark that attested to an almost-healed wound on Sarah's right hand, though she knew there had been no mark there earlier in the night.

The fact that the new injury, no doubt the source of the blood on the floor, was nearly closed scared Adianna more than anything had since their father had died. No witch healed that fast.

Her power flared as she knelt by her sister's side. She was dangerously close to losing control, but she knew of nothing on earth that would make her pause to regain it.

Sarah's skin was hot to the touch, and Adianna clamped her jaws tight as she saw the faint blush of blood on Sarah's mouth. Reaching out with a tendril of magic, she found the poison in Sarah's system.

They had given her their blood. Whether they had intended to blood bond her or to end her life did not matter. Sarah was a Daughter of Vida; her witch blood would destroy the invading vampiric blood, and probably destroy the body it was inside in the process.

A healer might have been able to do something, but any healer would have consulted Dominique before treating Sarah, and Dominique would have told them to let her die. Adianna would have to try on her own.

She knew what the consequences could be. This had not been attempted since Jade Arun had tried to heal her young daughter thousands of years ago. Since then every witch in the Arun line had been born with vampire blood. But if that was the price, Adianna would pay it.

She placed her hand over Sarah's feverish brow, closed her eyes, and tried to sever the bonds the vampiric blood had already made on Sarah's flesh.

She knew from the start it was a lost cause. The infection was too deep, and it had leached onto Sarah's blood too firmly.

"Damn it, Sarah!" Adianna's own shriek startled her back to the real world. "Don't you *dare* die on me. Do you hear me? Don't you *dare*." The last words were whispered, as she threw her mind and magic headlong into the swift tide that was Sarah's power.

The effect was similar to jumping into freezing river rapids headfirst, bogged down by pockets full of stones, with salt in her eyes, and every inch of skin raw to the bone. First she severed the ties Dominique's magic had fastened over Sarah's, and then steeled herself for her next move.

Sarah's magic was killing her as it killed the vampire blood. If Adianna could not pull out the vampiric toxin, then the only thing she could do was cut away the magic that was fighting it.

She was in Sarah's mind as well as in her magic, and even though she did not want to hear, she knew the truth. She could save Sarah's life by destroying her magic, but she knew quite clearly that her sister would rather die.

She held Sarah's life and magic between two fingertips. She could snap each with a thought.

Instead, trembling, she withdrew, breath dragging through her lungs with difficulty. The sun had completely risen while she had been drowning in Sarah's power, and she knew that the faint, cool sensation of someone's aura brushing over her was not new. He must have been there for hours, kneeling silently, slightly behind her and to her left.

She turned slowly, drawing the knife from her wrist as she did so, and he did not move to stop her.

"How is she?" Christopher asked, his voice soft.

Her voice cut as sharply as could her blade. "How did you think she would be after you gave her your blood? She is going to die."

Christopher's carefully neutral expression crumbled. The vampire leaned back against the wall and his eyes closed for a moment.

"I didn't think," Christopher answered quietly, raising his black gaze to meet the hunter's. "I lost control."

Adianna was Dominique Vida's older daughter. She had always been the strong sister, the one who honored the line, the one who made Dominique proud. She, more than anyone, knew exactly how much could be destroyed by losing control even for a few moments. She could also see how painful the confession was to the vampire.

Perhaps seeing Adianna's reluctant understanding, Christopher added, "I love her, and I never meant to hurt her. And I *will not* let her die because I screwed up." Though he spoke softly, Christopher's voice was rich with self-directed anger.

He stepped toward Sarah, and without thinking, Adianna moved between the vampire and her sister. "Get away from her."

"You're Sarah's sister," Christopher said,

his voice tight. "Do you really want her to die?"

Adianna flinched at the accusation; her nails bit crescents into her left palm as she clenched her hand into a fist. "How do you intend to help her?" she asked, but she knew the answer.

"I took her blood, and possibly her life," Christopher said. "It's only right if I give her mine." The meaning was clear. He meant to change her, to make her into one of the creatures that Sarah had spent her whole life hunting. Christopher must have seen some sign of revulsion in Adianna's face because he added, "She would be alive."

"She would be a . . ."

"Yes, she would be a vampire," Christopher snapped. "But she would be *alive*. Isn't that all that matters? I would prefer to change her and risk having her hate me even more for it than to let her die without giving her a choice."

Adianna could not agree. To allow her own sister to be turned into one of their kind would be worse than letting her die.

Before Adianna could raise the protest, Christopher calmed his voice and added, "If she wakes up and doesn't want it, Sarah is strong enough to fall on the knife. At least this way she *will* wake up."

Adianna choked on her own argument, and turned away from Christopher and Sarah. "Do what you have to do." Her voice broke on the words.

She stepped aside, but could not force her gaze away. Her resolve almost broke as the leech bared Sarah's throat; she leaned back against the wall and sank to the floor.

Get out of here, hunter. You don't want to watch this. The vampire's voice in her mind was loud, strengthened by the witch blood he had in him. Adianna felt the bile rise in her throat.

She stood, and turned her back on the pair. One step, two. She was almost at the door when, like Orpheus, she had to take one last glance—just in time to see Christopher draw his knife across his own skin, and to see Sarah latch on to the new wound like a suckling child.

Adianna lost control, and sprinted the rest of the way to her car. Twenty minutes later she convinced herself to slow down when she found herself pushing ninety-five on the highway; no matter how far or how fast she traveled, Adianna knew she would never outrun that last image.

From this night on, whether she chose to live as a vampire or kill herself, Sarah was as good as dead. Adianna prayed she would never see her sister again.

CHAPTER 29

AT SUNSET, Kristopher still sat by Sarah's side, waiting anxiously for her to stir.

Had he been too late? He cursed himself for wasting time arguing with the hunter, but he doubted that Sarah would have forgiven him if he had hurt Adianna. His system still hummed with the power of Sarah's witch blood, and if he had fought the hunter he probably would have killed her out of reflex.

His brother was pacing in the back of the room, his power crackling around him like a net of sparks, and as always Kristopher could feel the connection between them. Nikolas had a right to be there; they were in his house. It had been the only location that Kristopher had trusted to be safe enough.

A less intrusive presence, Nissa waited calmly in one of the other chairs. He wasn't sure why his sister was there—maybe to diffuse the situation if Sarah woke up hating him.

He brushed a long black hair from his face, the only movement he had made in almost twenty minutes, and glanced briefly at the abstract black-and-white clock on the wall. The sun should have set by now. She should have awakened.

Finally, Sarah moaned lightly, and Christopher's guilt came around to hit him again as he heard the pain in her tone. He knew that a newborn vampire, before she had ever hunted, was wracked by bloodlust so strong it could drive reason completely from the mind. Without killing, it was almost impossible to sate that hunger.

Sarah moaned again and sat up slowly, blinking to clear her vision. They all knew her mind was foggy. Her memory might not even return until after she fed. Kristopher and Nikolas both reached to help her up.

Sarah could barely stand on her own, and

she leaned on Kristopher as he held her. "I need to bring her someplace she can feed safely," he told his sister. Once Sarah had fed she would probably hate him. Worse, she might put her own knife through her heart.

Nissa stepped forward and put a hand on his shoulder. "Don't let her kill anyone, Kristopher."

Nikolas laughed, and Nissa flinched at the cutting tone. "That's impossible, Nissa. She's a new fledgling, and her change wasn't nearly as easy as yours was—if she doesn't take a life, she won't be able to sate the bloodlust, and you well know it."

"She's a Daughter of Vida. She won't take a human life," Nissa argued.

Nikolas looked at Sarah doubtfully as Kristopher gently smoothed a hand down her silky hair, trying to comfort her as much as he could while his siblings argued.

"I'll take her," Nissa said, her voice strong. "There are people I know at SingleEarth who will be willing."

Kristopher mirrored his brother's expression, doubtful. "Not willing to die." Like his sister, Kristopher had gone through the change easily; only Nikolas had woken to the mind-numbing pain that Sarah was going through.

Nikolas and Nissa continued to argue, but Kristopher had already made a decision. Human blood was too weak to sate the bloodlust without a kill. Witch blood would have been best, since it was strong enough to quench the thirst without killing the donor, but every instinct rebelled against bringing Sarah to her kin. The witches answered to Dominique, and Dominique was the last person who could know what had become of her daughter.

There was only one choice left—had always been only one choice. Tilting his head back, he drew Sarah to his own throat.

CHAPTER 30

GODDESS, IT HURT. Fire and glass were being forced through her veins and she could do nothing about it.

Drink, she heard in her mind, and suddenly she was aware of the sweet scent that filled her senses.

Sarah's instincts took over as Kristopher pulled her to his own throat. Graceful as any predator, she wrapped a hand around the back of his neck and sealed her lips over the pulse point. She felt the weight of her own fangs in her mouth, the moment of resistance as they pierced the skin, and then only the rich, warm blood that flowed over her tongue.

Then there was only the sweet, rich taste, and a million images that accompanied it. She was not prepared for the flood of memories and emotions, but she understood that Kristopher could not have blocked her from his mind if he had tried. Not while she was this close, not while his blood flowed past her lips.

Some of the memories were pleasant, some harsh, and as she flickered among them she lost track of her own self.

"Nicholas, or Christopher?" the girl asked with a toss of her golden curls. Dressed in pale cream, with an ivy wreath and a white rose in her lap, Christine Brunswick was every inch the May Queen. He flinched at the question, but it was common enough. Only from Christine did it have the power to cut.

Power like lightening struck him, knocking him away from their willing prey. Pain worse than even the searing torture of the bloodlust, as Elisabeth Vida's knife sank into his chest, only missing his heart because his brother had hit the witch's arm.

He thought he was going to die, like this, but somehow they got the knife out. The witch's blood was sweeter than the richest honey, and the pain dimmed as he took it, with his brother beside him.

He remembered when the human world had found her body. The names Nikolas and Kristopher had been on the lips of the world that they had lost. Christopher Ravena—the name he had been given when he was born—was not a hunter, and so he had changed the name when he signed it on his prey. Such a small change, but a symbol of his difference, the last break he had made from the world he had been born in.

Nissa, at one of their bashes, the first time the brothers had seen her since they had been changed a hundred years before. She was nervous of Kaleo and the others, but eventually she relaxed in the heady atmosphere of predatory contentment. No one here hid his nature.

One human got out of hand and made the mistake of insulting Nissa while her brothers looked on. He never would have lived through the night, and Nissa had known that. The Devil's Hour fell, and no one thought to stop Nissa as she bared the man's throat and fed.

Nissa, dying as she refused to feed again. Dying as her own guilt tore her apart. He wasn't sure he could survive without Nikolas, but he knew Nissa couldn't live without him. Later, when she was strong again, he could go back to his brother, but right now . . . she needed him.

Even before he spoke to her, he adored her. Her beauty, her grace, and the thoughtful expression she wore that told him she was not listening to a thing the teacher was saying . . . all of that enthralled him. After he spoke to her, after he had laughed with her and learned about her, he could not have helped being fascinated by her. She was too polished, too impossible, and he kept wondering what lay beneath.

Sarah Tigress Vida, youngest Daughter of Vida. Finally he understood the strength he had seen in her. And only then, when she told him to leave her alone, did he realize that he loved her.

Fighting the desire to argue, he had fallen back into the neutral mask Kristopher wore when he was not in friendly territory. He wanted to kiss her, but instead he had been cold, because otherwise he would not have been able to keep himself from asking her to defy all the rules. He would never ask her to give up so much, not for him.

When the spell finally broke and Sarah stepped back, the hunger and the pain were gone, but a duality remained. Though Sarah tried to ignore the sensation, it was like turning her back to a conversation. The direct thoughts and memories disappeared, but there remained a lingering sense of Kristopher's mind.

Kristopher stepped back, and Sarah knew that he would have blocked the connection, if it had been his decision. The wound that Christine had left was still healing. He had adored Christine; she had been the most beautiful woman he had ever seen. The last thing he wanted was for Sarah to see what Christine had been to him.

"Kristopher?" The question came from Nikolas, who had been standing quietly at the other side of the room.

Kristopher shook his head as if to clear his mind. "I'm . . . fine," he answered finally. Forcibly turning his mind from the memories, he raised his gaze to Sarah's and said simply, "What you do now is your choice."

He was not going to mention it aloud, but she could easily feel his fear, and she understood it. He was worried that she was going to kill herself.

But if she didn't, what could she do? Her life and everything she had known were gone. Her own mother would kill her if she tried to go back.

A true Vida would have fallen on the knife the moment she had become a vampire, but Sarah did not want to die. She had made friends with Nissa, and with Christopher, and they had taught her that the vampire blood did not turn a person into a monster.

CHAPTER 31

WHEN SHE GAVE NO RESPONSE, Kristopher took a breath. After a hesitation that told her he was bracing himself for her answer, he said, "Sarah, I don't give a damn about your past—I love you. If you want to, you're welcome to stay with us."

She saw Nikolas's surprise when he heard the "us," but the vampire didn't argue. The idea gave Sarah pause, however.

If the "us" had meant Christopher and Nissa, she would have said yes immediately. But she knew how Nikolas lived, how he hunted. He killed, and whether his prey was willing or not didn't matter to Sarah. She couldn't live that way.

Before she could voice her refusal, Nikolas spoke.

"Sarah . . ." He paused and looked to Kristopher for a moment before he continued, as if for approval. "I'm not expecting your instant forgiveness. I'm not even asking for it." He started to take a step in her direction, but then seemed to think better of it and stopped. "But if nothing else, trust me when I say I won't ever hurt my brother, or let him be hurt if I can stop it." Again he glanced at his brother, but this time only for a moment, as if he already knew how Kristopher would react. "We don't own you. Whatever you choose today . . . I'm no threat to you. But don't blame Kristopher for what I've done, and don't leave just because I'm here."

Sarah opened her mouth to disagree, but then closed it as Nikolas's words sank in. Her instinct was to argue with anything he said, but right now what he said made sense.

She couldn't stay, but it wasn't because of Nikolas. Quite abruptly she realized that her hatred for him seemed to have faded. Her brush with Kristopher's mind had caused some of that; it was nearly impossible to completely hate Nikolas once she had felt the intense love and loyalty Kristopher held for his brother.

Yes, he had hurt her physically, but pain was only fleeting. Honestly, the most brutal thing Nikolas had done to her had been to open her eyes and force her to see reality — the shades of gray that existed in the world, beyond the world of stark black and white, of evil and good, that Dominique had taught her long ago.

She took a breath, but her mind was made up. "I can't stay," she said finally, and she saw — and felt — Kristopher flinch. "You know I can't survive — and hunt — the same way you do. Even if I could, I don't like to be dependent. Give me some time to find my own way to live." She lifted her gaze and met Kristopher's. His fear, which was still ringing clear in her mind, prompted her to add, "I don't hate you, Kristopher. I don't hate you or your brother." On a burst of impulsiveness that would have made Dominique cringe, she stepped forward and hugged him. "I'll miss you, Kristopher, but I can't stay here. For now at least."

"We have forever. I'll see you again," he answered with certainty. "But before you go—"

Kristopher tilted her face up and kissed her.

It occurred to Sarah then that she had never been kissed, really kissed, before.

However, as first kisses went . . .

Like all of Kristopher's art, his kisses were expertly done.

Kristopher was the one who broke the kiss, though he kept his arms around her and did not pull back far. "I'm sorry. I've wanted to do that for"—he shrugged—"too long."

"That is a moment you never need to apologize for."

He smiled, and in the expression Sarah saw the true Christopher, whom she had come to know and trust.

"There are a million other moments, both past and future, that I should apologize to you for," he said lightly. "I might as well start earning credit."

A million moments, both past and future. Thousands of years of hatred, between both their kinds, could hardly be undone quickly. Even in the eternity that she potentially had ahead of her, she didn't think she was up to a job as a peacemaker. But if she had been . . .

SingleEarth would take her in if she asked. Nissa could teach her how to survive without killing. There were pockets of peace in the world, and if she could just find one of them, she could make a life there. As Kristopher had pointed out, she had forever.

ABOUT THE AUTHOR

AMELIA ATWATER-RHODES lives in Concord, Massachusetts, with her family. Born in 1984, she wrote her first novel, *In the Forests of the Night*, at age thirteen and her second novel, *Demon in My View*, an ALA Quick Pick for Young Adults, just two years later. Named one of the 20 Teens Who Will Change the World by *Teen People*, Atwater-Rhodes has been featured in *Seventeen*, *USA Today*, *Entertainment Weekly*, and *The New Yorker* and has appeared on *The Rosie O'Donnell Show* and *CBS This Morning*. *In the Forests of the Night* has been praised as "remarkable" (*Voice of Youth Advocates*) and "mature and polished" (*Booklist*), while *Publishers Weekly* has praised *Demon in My View* as a book "readers will drain . . . in one big gulp."